mYS inho

Babson, Marian

Pretty lady

PRETTY LADY

Also by Marian Babson

PRETTY LADY

Marian Babson

Walker and Company
New York

First published in the United States of America in 1990
by Walker Publishing Company, Inc.

Library of Congress Cataloging-in-Publication Data

Babson, Marian.
Pretty lady / Marian Babson.
ISBN 0-8027-5778-2
I. Title.
PS3552.A25P74   1990
813'.54—dc20   90-38046

Printed in the United States of America

2   4   6   8   10   9   7   5   3   1

MERELDA

She had stopped thinking of him as human. What she had to do was easier that way.

Not that she would have considered doing such a thing had he left her any other choice, but he had not. He had forced her into it.

In the full glare of the lights around the mirror, she sat at her make-up table and considered her face with professional detachment. It was good for a few years yet. Perhaps . . . very few.

After that, a few more years, leaning heavily on the soft focus technique – the modern equivalent of the old-fashioned method of filming through a gauze veil. She remembered once hearing someone remark about an ageing star. 'Shooting her through a veil? They're shooting that broad through linoleum, these days.'

She had laughed at the time. It didn't seem so funny any more. A lot of things had changed in the past year or so.

Five years ago, it had seemed ideal. A wealthy marriage, a devoted husband – there were worse fates than being an old man's darling. After years in a bedsitter, doing the rounds of management offices, auditions, a day's filming here and there, she'd known most of them.

It had been bliss to relax into the cushioned nest of luxury, limousines, and charge accounts. Actually, he needn't even have bothered to marry her. Of course, she hadn't let him know that, once she realized the direction his thoughts were taking. A wife was in a much more impregnable position than a mistress. All the laws of the land were on her side – including the law of inheritance.

Had that thought been at the back of her mind, even so long ago as that?

No, she'd tried, honestly tried. Through endless dinner parties, with his dull northern industrialist friends eyeing her speculatively, and their dumpy dreary little wives – suspicious and unfriendly – making it clear that they felt Keith had married beneath him. Making it so clear that his early promises of financing a film for her had been allowed to fade, as he began to hope she'd forget the past – and that all his friends would forget it, too.

Not that his background was so marvellous. He was a 'self-made' man and, like them all, boasted about it till he had driven his audience to the point of nausea. But to marry someone from the theatre! To them, he'd have done better to pick a wife out of the gutter – they'd have considered her a better class.

Her own friends, like her career, had slipped away imperceptibly. Keith hadn't liked them and her fear of his displeasure had been stronger in those days. They hadn't liked him, either. In self-defence, their voices had grown shriller, their gestures more sweeping, their mockery of his mannerisms and accent more blatant, more cruel.

Afraid of losing her new-found security, she had grown cool towards them, let the time between invitations grow longer, the notes on Christmas cards shorter. She hadn't realized how much she had missed them, how desperate she had been growing to be with her own kind.

Until she met Nick again.

That meeting had suddenly crystallized all the discontent she hadn't realized had been building up in her. The restlessness, the resentment, the . . . ego.

Sitting in the little pub off Wardour Street, laughing, talking, catching up with the old gossip, the course she had to take became clear to her.

She'd sworn to Nick that she was happy, of course, accepted his congratulations on the way life had been treating her, and promised that they'd get together again soon. She'd managed to escape without giving him a time or place. She'd call him . . . later.

Nick mustn't be involved in what she had to do.

There'd be time to get in touch with Nick again . . . later. And with the others.

She didn't need him now.

What she needed now was a . . . catspaw.

DENNY

Denny was a good boy. Denny went to church on Sundays. Sometimes Denny went during the week, too. It was quiet in church and smelled of flowers and the ghost of incense. The candles were bright and glowing, drawing him to them. You mustn't play with fire, he knew. Sometimes, if he had enough pocket money, he lit a candle himself. That wasn't playing with fire. That was allowed.

He frowned into the mirror, then scrubbed harder behind his ears. Mum always checked them, and he wasn't allowed to go out to play unless he was absolutely clean. It took a lot of time, she was so fussy. And she always noticed if he skimped on soap and water anywhere. It was a nuisance on a day like this.

The sun was shining. He could hear birds singing. He knew where there was a bird's nest with eggs just about ready to hatch out. If there was no one watching, he could climb up and see if the baby birds were out of their shells yet. But not if anyone was watching. He wouldn't hurt the baby birds, he'd just look at them, but bad boys robbed nests, hurt the baby birds. That was why he must be very careful not to lead anyone to the secret nest.

Maybe he could find somebody to play with, too. Everyone around here seemed to go away for the school holidays. It was too bad that he couldn't go, too. It was lonely sometimes without the other kids around. Sometimes he missed them.

He even missed Mary-Maureen. Although she played too rough, and lost her temper and pushed if you didn't let her win. And he couldn't push back. Boys didn't push girls, it wasn't nice. Boys didn't push other boys, either, as they got bigger. It was something to do with growing up and learning to get on with other people. Mum had explained it to him – it was something else she was awfully fussy about.

He hadn't seen Mary-Maureen for a long time now. Longer than before school holidays started, even. She had gone away, Mum said. Mary-Maureen wasn't feeling well and she had gone away for a while. ('Now stop asking those endless questions—that's all there is to it!')

He *must* be clean enough now. He picked up the nail-brush and scrubbed in desperation at his nails. How did they always get so black?

'Denny,' his mother's voice came floating up the stairs to him. 'Breakfast's ready, Denny.'

He mopped up hastily with the hand towel. How did everything get so splashed? If he didn't leave things clean and tidy behind him, he wasn't allowed to go out until they were. It was fair, he knew. Mum couldn't do every-thing, and he had to help her. He was a big boy now.

'Denny,' she called again. This wasn't one of the days when she could be kept waiting. Sheila had already had her breakfast and left for work, he knew. He had heard her cheery 'Goodbye' and the slam of the door while he was still sitting on the side of his bed, planning what he was going to do today. '*Dreaming*,' his mother would have called it.

He clattered down the stairs, then checked himself midway and descended slowly. If Mum wasn't feeling well, noise upset her. Somehow, it seemed to be easier to upset her these days. Sometimes, most times, he didn't even know what he had done.

She looked up and smiled as he came into the kitchen. 'Good morning, Denny.'

He relaxed a bit. 'Good morning, Mum.' It might be going to be one of her good days. He pulled out his chair and sat down, pulling his plate towards him.

'Denny,' warningly, 'manners.'

'Sorry, Mum.' Carefully, he sat up straight, shook out his napkin and laid it across his lap.

'That's better.' She poured his tea. 'Don't eat too fast.'

He slowed down, but he wasn't going fast. Not dipping fingers of toast into boiled egg. Mum got too upset if any bit of yolk dribbled on to his shirt. She made him change his shirt. Sometimes she cried. He was always extra careful with boiled eggs.

'I'm working at the hospital today, Denny,' she reminded him. 'Have you got your latchkey?'

Mouth full, he nodded vigorously, groping with his free hand for the key suspended against his chest by the thin metal chain around his neck. He always put it on first thing every morning. He had used to have a Miraculous Medal on the chain, too. He'd liked the friendly noise they made, jingling together, as he walked along. Bad boys had laughed, though. They made jokes about licensing him like a dog. He hadn't minded. But Mum had heard them. Now he wore a soft cloth scapular under his shirt instead.

'All right, Denny,' Mum said. 'Leave it where it is. Long as you have it. I've packed you a nice lunch. Why don't you eat it in the park?'

He nodded agreement, not really meaning it, but it wasn't a lie if he didn't *say* anything. The park was fine, but the river was better.

There were ducklings along the river now. New, fluffy, funny little things – soft and trusting. They came swarming to the bank, begging for scraps and darting to gobble them up, getting in each other's way, making him laugh.

He looked around quickly. Mum's back was turned. He snatched the last two pieces of toast from the plate, folding them over and stuffing them into his pocket. There were so many ducklings – there was never enough bread in his sandwiches to satisfy them all.

'Don't stay out too late, now,' his mother went on. 'Sheila will be back and give you your tea, if I'm not home.'

He nodded, no reservations about his agreement this time. Sheila cut bigger slices of cake than Mum. Sometimes she let him eat her piece, too. He wished sometimes he had a brother, but, if he had to have a sister, Sheila was as good as anyone could want.

'Are you all right, then, Denny?' his mother asked, as he pushed back his chair.

He nodded again, then said quickly, 'Yes, Mum,' fore-stalling her frown. It upset her, if he didn't talk to her enough.

He washed his hands hastily at the kitchen sink, dabbed the towel quickly across his mouth. The sun seemed to grow brighter by the moment, beckoning him to come outdoors.

'All right, now, is your shirt clean? Your collar?'

He stood, fidgeting, for her inspection. It was necessary before he could break free of the house.

'Your ears? Your fingernails?'

He held his hands out for her inspection, knowing she could not fault him there.

'All right.' She gave approval at last. 'Be careful crossing streets, Denny. Don't play with the rough boys. Don't speak to strangers – '

He nodded as she continued the familiar litany, shrug-ging himself into his coat. She followed him to the door, watching him as he picked up the airline bag Sheila had brought back from last year's holiday and checked his treasures.

All there, with the generous packet of sandwiches and biscuits on top. An apple and a banana, too. He straight-ened up with it, sending her a brilliant smile of thanks.

'Oh, Denny, Denny!' He watched in panic as the tears came to her eyes. He'd thought it was going to be a good day with her.

He stood frozen with horror and sympathy, feeling his own eyes begin to fill. What was the matter? He'd tried to be so careful not to do anything to upset her. He hadn't done anything bad. Denny was a good boy.

'Ah, Denny, you're a good boy.' She said it then, patting his arm.

He smiled uneasily, wriggling in his anxiety to get away. But there was one more bit of the morning ritual he must wait for. Mum got upset if he didn't. It was sissy, but it was different for ladies. Mum was a lady. He opened the front door and stood there, waiting.

'Be good, Denny.' As usual, she kissed him goodbye.

Standing, as always, on tiptoe to brush her lips across the point of his chin.

POLLY

The tall figure marching proudly down the path to the front gate, swinging his airline bag, shimmered in a misty halo for a moment, then disappeared completely into a blur.

She tugged the handkerchief from the cleft between her breasts and dabbed at her eyes briskly. It had been a long time since she'd cried over Denny, but tears were always closer now. They came with the pain, and the physical pain and the mental anguish blended together indistinguishably until she couldn't tell which the tears were for. Only that they were suddenly there.

She must try to control them – they frightened Denny. Poor Denny. It wasn't his fault. He tried so hard, he was such a good boy, God love him.

(*God love him and receive him. As He will never receive me.*)

She heard the creak of the gate and waved automatically, knowing that Denny would have turned to wave to her. She stepped back and closed the door, moving slowly, carefully, so that the pain coiled in her vitals might not be disturbed to strike again. It was always worse when she hadn't slept well, but she had saved last night's sleeping pill, putting it in the hidden bottle with the others so carefully hoarded. Perhaps she should have let herself take it. Tonight she would go back to the doctor and get the prescription renewed again. For the last time.

It would be hard on Sheila, of course, but not so hard as the alternative. Poor Sheila, so good, so uncomplaining.

Accepting the situation as soon as she was old enough
to understand it, and helping take care of Denny as though
she were the older of the two. As, in a way, she was.

Strange, the way things turned out. Incomprehensible.
There was Denny – so longed for, so waited for, so wel-
comed with pride. And look at the way he had come to
them – unfinished.

She and Brian, in their pride, had not noticed it for
a long time. So fine to have a son. Such a bouncing, bonny
baby – a perfect physical specimen.

At first, it was just the little things – hardly noticeable
when you didn't know what to look for. When you never
suspected anything could be wrong. He was always a bit
behind the other babies his age, a bit slower to walk, to
talk. ('*Ah, but he'll catch up,*' she and Brian told themselves, '*and then there'll be no stopping him. He'll show all
those others a clean pair of heels!*')

Gradually, they'd stopped saying it. Imperceptibly, the
realization grew in them, even before they took him to
the hospital for that great battery of tests which only con-
firmed what they already knew.

There would be no catching up for Denny. Not ever. He
would go just so far – and always more slowly than the
other children of his age – until, finally, he reached the
point beyond which he could not go. He would remain
there, a placid, friendly, smiling child. A little boy, her little
boy – for ever.

And then there was Sheila – an accident. After Denny,
they knew there should be no other. So they closed their
eyes and their ears and their hearts to God and tried to
ensure that there should not be. One like Denny was
enough for any mortal parents to bear. But the accident
happened just the same.

A stubborn little accident. With all the emetics and the
jumping off tables and the hot gin and hotter baths not
able to dislodge her.

It was God's own mercy that she hadn't been damaged
far worse than Denny, with all that nonsense.

But Sheila was a blessing. One they didn't deserve, perhaps, but what would they have done without her? Sheila proved, too, that Denny wasn't their fault; that there wasn't a fatal strain of bad blood in either her or Brian that would doom all their children to the endless childhood that was Denny's.

('*God's will*,' the priests said, feebly proffering the only explanation they had for the inexplicable. But why drag God into a terrible thing like that?)

It was nature. Just one of the cruel capricious pranks of nature. It might not have been so bad, even, if poor Denny had been stunted in some other way, as well – a midget, or a dwarf. (Not that she'd wish a thing like that on him.) But, in some funny way, it would have been easier to bear. Perhaps because people would have been forewarned. As it was, he had a man's body – an athlete's, almost – and the feckless, wandering mind of a child.

There was no use brooding about it. She moved slowly back to the kitchen and the breakfast dishes waiting in the sink. She must do those before she left the house. It wasn't fair to leave them for Sheila to find when she came home from work. Sheila did enough.

Sheila. Funny, after they'd been sure Sheila was normal, they'd relaxed, she and Brian. Ready to welcome another child or two, but none had come. There was only Sheila, who had grown up so quickly, and Denny, who would never grow up at all.

The tears and the pain came simultaneously again. She took a deep breath, willing herself to learn how to control them. She mustn't keep letting poor Denny see tears. They frightened him into inarticulate misery, standing there in front of her, with those poor dumb eyes asking, '*What can I do?*'

What would he do when there was no one left to tell him?

(*Denny, Denny, don't be afraid.* She drew a deep breath against the ravenous pain. *I won't leave you, Denny. I won't leave you behind.*)

DENNY

He walked faster as he got farther away from the house. It was going to be a nice day, the sun was warm already. Later, he might take his coat off, remembering to put it on again before he got home. Sheila wouldn't tattle on him, but some of the neighbours might.

He turned the corner, moving farther into freedom. He looked around cautiously. No one was in sight, no curtain twitched in any window fronting on the street. It was safe, there was no one watching.

He gave a skip, and then another, skipping all the way to the next corner. He stopped abruptly then, you never could tell who might be around the corner. Someone to catch him and tell Mum. He'd like to run and jump on a day like this, but it wasn't allowed. Mum had explained to him. Big boys didn't do things like that. Denny was a big boy now.

Denny was a good boy, too. So he must behave himself properly. Like a big boy.

Denny frowned. Somehow, he'd expected things to be different when he was a big boy. But everything was just the same. Maybe all big boys still felt the same inside, no matter how big they got. But some of them couldn't, because they behaved differently.

He'd like to. But Mum wouldn't let him grew a beard or wear his hair long. Only . . . only . . . there was something more than that to it. There was getting a job and going to work every day.

'Sure, Denny, don't worry your head over that,' Mum always said. It was what she said about a lot of things. He didn't worry, exactly, but there were a lot of things he'd like to know, because he didn't quite understand . . .

But it was too good a day to think about hard things. Rainy days, when you couldn't go outdoors and had to sit inside and watch the raindrops sliding down the window-

pane, were the best days for trying to figure out the hard
things. Not good days. Today was a good day.

Today was such a good day he might even find Rembrandt. He quickened his steps, wondering where to start
looking. Rembrandt was never in the same place twice. Not
very often. The police didn't like him to be.

'*Move along, move along,*' Rembrandt had said. '*Those
are the first words a copper learns to say. But that
wouldn't bother you, would it, Denny? You like moving
along, don't you, Denny? One place is as good as another
to you.*'

Denny had grinned and followed Rembrandt, helping by
carrying some of the pictures. He didn't always understand
what Rembrandt meant by some of the things he said, but
he liked Rembrandt. Rembrandt was his friend.

It was too bad Rembrandt had to leave some of his
pictures behind every time he moved. Sunsets and sailing
ships and kittens and doggies, all done swiftly with coloured
chalks on the pavement. '*Penny catchers,*' Rembrandt
had called them, with a funny sneer in his voice. But Denny
liked them best. He didn't say so, though, because of the
way Rembrandt looked and sounded when he talked
about them. Rembrandt liked the strange dark shapes on
the canvases best.

You could tell right away what some of them were – like
the places along the river – even though they were sort
of dark and shadowy. But the other pictures were frightening – full of things you couldn't quite see, but knew were
there in the darker shapes of the shadows. Things from
nightmares and fevers, lurking to spring at you if you
weren't watchful. Rembrandt knew which ones frightened
him most and, when he saw him coming, he turned them
around the other way, to face the building. Rembrandt was
a good friend.

He'd tried to tell Mum about Rembrandt once, but
she'd gone all funny and explained carefully that Rembrandt was dead, had been dead a long time. Later, he'd
heard her say to Sheila, '*Where do you suppose he picked
all that up from?*'

Big boys don't cry. So he'd gone to his room and bitten
down hard on his knuckles – until he'd drawn blood,
almost. And he'd been sad for a long while to think that his
friend Rembrandt was dead. So sad he'd avoided the
places where Rembrandt used to be.

Until, one day, turning an unfamiliar corner, he'd found
him again. Alive and choosing a tawny gold chalk to finish
the cocker spaniel 'penny catcher'. Denny had been too
glad to speak. He just stood there, beaming, while the
great black stone rolled off his chest. Mum wasn't right
about everything, after all. Rembrandt was still alive.

'*Hello, there, Denny,*' Rembrandt had looked up.
'*Haven't seen you for a long time. Where have you been
keeping yourself? Had the 'flu, or something?*'

Because he couldn't find all the words he wanted to say,
and because he probably couldn't say them anyway past
the lump in his throat (*big boys don't cry*), Denny had just
nodded.

He was still glad, when he thought about it, that Mum
had been wrong. Even though he couldn't quite understand how – she had never been wrong about anybody
being dead before. If she said they were dead, they were.
And she put on her hat and took Denny, and went down to
the parish house and got a Mass Card for the repose of
their souls.

Perhaps he'd got the name wrong. It would be easy to,
because every time he'd asked Rembrandt his name
when he first knew him, Rembrandt had said something
different.

'*Rembrandt,*' he'd said, with a funny twist to his mouth.
'*Vermeer. Holbein. Botticelli. Gainsborough. Titian.
"What's in a name?" Call me anything you like, Denny.*'

Denny had understood. Sometimes, when he was
younger, he'd had trouble remembering his own name
himself. It was nice to meet a grown-up with the same
problem. It made them better friends, in a way.

'*Rembrandt,*' he'd decided. He liked the sound of it. He
liked Rembrandt and all the bits of broken coloured chalks
Rembrandt gave him for his treasure bag.

He walked along briskly, not quite skipping, the good feeling building up inside of him. He was going to find Rembrandt today. On the good days, all the nicest things happened. And finding Rembrandt was one of the nicest things he knew.

MERELDA

He sat across the breakfast table, looking sickeningly satisfied with himself, and beamed at her. As well he might. She didn't dare lock her door to him. He must not suspect anything, there must never be any suggestion of discord which he might hint at to his friends.

She kept her face smooth, her smile bland, willing herself not to think, to play the scene. It was Act 1, Scene 1 of any English drawing-room comedy. Morning in a sunny breakfast room. The smiling, serene heroine and her bumbling husband.

She must think of it as just another long-running show. Not that she had ever been in any. But she must smile and play the role for just a little longer. Consoling herself with the knowledge that the run was ending soon.

It would be easier, though, with another face across the breakfast table from her. Peter O'Toole, perhaps. Or Albert Finney. Or . . . Nick.

'What are you doing today, love?'

It was the second time he had asked that. She came out of her reverie with a start. She must be more careful. She must keep paying attention. Otherwise, one missed one's cues, lost one's . . . audience. She smiled warmly at him.

'Harrods, I thought. I'll need something new for the Brainnerds's bridge party. I might get a dress . . . or a suit.'

'Buy both!' he said expansively. How he exulted in letting her spend money. In the power he felt at commanding an expensive wife. He felt the same about the Rolls — he liked sleek, well-maintained status symbols.

'Perhaps I shall.' She made a face at him. 'That will teach you!'

She controlled her inward wince as his laugh boomed out. It wasn't wasted. The maid entered just then with the morning post. A valuable witness. ('Ever so happy, they always were, with their laughing and little jokes . . . right up to the last.')

'You'll be in town lunchtime, then?' he asked hopefully. She knew what that meant – lunch at his dreary club. On display, captured by his prowess, the young exotic wife – that his associates might envy him. *That* was a role she was tired of, too.

'Happen you might meet me for lunch? At t'club?'

The maid was still lingering, listening. She kept her faint protest perfunctory, as though she didn't mean it. ('It was more like a joke, really. She never meant it for a minute. She'd never have said such a thing, even joking, if she'd only known . . .')

'T'club?' (Careful, nearly mocked the accent that time – mustn't get too close to the knuckle . . . not now.) 'With that great stodgy menu? They don't believe in salads there, do they? . . . Or diets?'

'Some place else, then?' But his face shadowed slightly – all his friends ate at the club. 'Anywhere you like, love.'

'No, no,' she laughed lightly. 'I won't deprive you of your roly-poly pud. I'll take a long walk afterwards and work it off.'

'Done!' He beamed at her and she smiled back, feeling the ache begin in her jaw from clenching her teeth too much.

The maid left them and she switched off her smile, consciously trying to relax her jaw. She mustn't let her nerves get the better of her. Not at this stage. Now that she had made the decision, however, it was hard to go on as before. But she must, while she tried to work out the details, to decide how it could be done with safety . . . for her.

Keith began reading his post, the smile still loitering

foolishly on his face. Why shouldn't it? He had everything *he* wanted. Money, and the power that went with
it, and . . . her.

He looked up, and she smiled quickly. That was part
of her job – and she *was* the best paid of his employees.
And, a bit more warmth crept into her smile, hers was
the best pension scheme. Widow's pension, of course.

'Nice day for a walk, looks like,' he said.

'All the flowers are coming out now,' she agreed. 'It
should be lovely . . . along the river.'

DENNY

There was a puppy frisking along on the other side of
the low hedge, whimpering for attention. Denny knew he
shouldn't stop to pat him. People came to their doors
sometimes and shouted at him when he did things like
that. Mum had explained it to him. Big boys didn't touch
other people's property.

Denny hesitated and looked over his shoulder. The
puppy, sensing victory, began a shrill high yapping, leaping
up as though determined to clear the hedge.

'Hello, boy!' Denny reached over the hedge, patting
the eager head. 'Hello, there.'

It was too bad Mum wouldn't let him have a dog.
He wouldn't take care of it properly, she said, and it would
just be more work for her, and God knew she had enough.

He *would* take care of a dog, though. He'd train it never
to chase birds or cats. And they could go for runs in the
park – even grown-ups were allowed to run when they had
a dog with them.

The puppy would love to come out for a run. His wistful
whimper told Denny so. If he was only a little bigger, he
could jump over the hedge. As it was, someone had to
open the gate for him before he could come out to play.

Denny's hand went to the gate, almost as though it had

a will of its own. The puppy watched, whining hopefully.

At the window, a curtain twitched suddenly. Denny's hand drew back. He knew what that meant. A movement of a curtain was followed by the window being flung up, or the door opening. In either case, people shouted at you.

Uneasily, Denny began to move along, the puppy moving with him to the end of the hedge, still hoping he'd change his mind. He could feel the unseen eyes following him, too, making sure he went away.

'That's a good boy, Denny.' He jumped as the familiar voice sounded at his elbow. He had been so intent upon the puppy that he hadn't seen Constable Pete approaching.

'Hello, Pete.' He couldn't quite shake off the guilty feeling. Had Pete known how close he'd come to letting the puppy out? To touching other people's property?

'It's a nice day for a walk.' Constable Pete fell into step beside him. 'Going far?'

'Going to feed the ducks,' Denny said.

'Ah.' Constable Pete nodded. 'By the lake, eh? Fine families of little ducklings they've got there this year.'

'By the river,' Denny said, already wondering whether he should go to the lake, instead. 'Lots of little ducklings.' Maybe he could go to the river tomorrow. Or maybe he ought to go to the lake tomorrow. He frowned, struggling to make the decision.

'I saw your artist friend, earlier,' Constable Pete said. 'He was setting up for business down in front of the Odeon Cinema.'

'Rembrandt?' Denny brightened, remembering that he had been hoping to find Rembrandt today.

'Is that the name he gave you?' Constable Pete laughed. 'Well, it's a good one, all right. They don't come much better. Maybe he's got the right idea.'

'Rembrandt is my friend,' Denny said proudly.

'We're all your friends, Denny,' Constable Pete said. 'Just you remember that.'

Denny nodded obligingly, stifling a sigh. There were always so many things people wanted him to remember.

'I turn off here, Denny. Have a good day.' Constable

Pete watched Denny safely off his beat, returning his
goodbye wave.

Good day. Denny walked faster. *The Odeon Cinema.*
That was where he'd find Rembrandt.

It was going to be a good day, after all.

POLLY

The waves of heat and food odours beat at her as she
moved slowly past the steam table in the hospital canteen.
It was a long slow queue and she gripped her tray tightly,
leaning on it under the guise of sliding it along the rails.

She had a milk pudding on her tray and, at the end of
the counter, she would collect a cup of tea. It was more
than she wanted, but she had to force herself to eat. She
had to keep going. For a while longer.

'Mrs O'Magnon, are you all right?' Teapot poised over
the empty cup, the canteen helper stared at her anxiously.

'Just a bit tired, that's all.' Polly tried to smile.

'Glory be to God! – that's never all you're eating? It
wouldn't keep a bird alive.'

'It's as much as I want right now.' Polly bit down on
her irritation. The woman meant well, there was no point
in taking it out on her. 'I'll be having a big tea when I get
home tonight.'

'Well . . .' Reluctantly, the woman tilted the teapot and
let the dark liquid pour into the waiting cup. 'If you're
sure . . .'

'I had a big breakfast, too,' Polly lied reassuringly. 'I'll
survive.' For a little while longer.

'I don't like your colour – and that's a fact. You're pale
as death.'

'I'm all right.' Polly reached out and firmly took the
cup of tea from her hand. With conscious effort, she
straightened and carried her tray to an unoccupied table in
the far corner of the canteen, walking briskly.

Once there, she sank into the chair limply, closing her

eyes. The spurts of effort cost more every time.

'You look like death-warmed-over.' The sharp voice cut at her. 'Are those pills doing you any good at all?'

'I'm all right.' She picked up her cup with both hands, steadying it against Vera's sharp, prying eyes. This was the second person within a few minutes to speak of death – was it written so prominently on her features already?

'Those pills,' Vera kept probing. 'Are you taking them the way you ought?'

'I have been.' She didn't look up. 'I've only just run out. I'll be going to the doctor's tonight and getting some more. Then I'll be fine.'

'You ought to ask him for something stronger. I don't believe those are helping at all. Make him give you something different. If you want my opinion – '

No one ever wanted Vera's opinion, but she gave it anyway. She was a good soul, basically.

'I think you ought to see Mr Brady.'

Mr Brady was a surgeon. Polly stiffened and saw the small sharp eyes sparkling as Vera realized she'd struck home.

'You've got to look after yourself, you know.'

Polly recognized her mood. Vera was determined to say her say. You could not tell Vera to mind her own business. She considered this her business. Vera had not only got her the job at the hospital, but she was Brian's eldest sister – the only one in this country.

Vera's interference was sanctioned by ties of family and friendship. Sometimes she pushed them too far. This was going to be one of those times.

'You've got to think of the children, you know.'

As though I thought of anything else. 'I do,' she said. Anyone else would have been warned off by her tone. But not Vera.

'How *is* poor Denny?' It was why she had come over, the subject she was determined to re-open and pursue. 'Is he any better?'

'He isn't any worse.' That was what Vera really wanted to know. Vera had never been able to reconcile herself to Denny's condition, had never brought herself to accept the fact that there would never be any change in it. There would be no great dramatic recovery in which Denny suddenly would achieve a forward stride to bring him into step with his generation. Nor would there be any rapid degeneration leading to debilitation and death. Denny was Denny – and always would be. He was perfectly happy in his own way, he was strong and healthy. He was just . . . wanting.

'Have you heard any more about that Mary-Maureen? How she is? Sure – ' Vera sighed deeply – 'that was a terrible thing. It was only God's own mercy the child didn't die.'

That was Vera's idea of being oblique, of subtly pointing out the dangers in allowing the mentally deficient to live among and associate with the rest of the community.

'Mary-Maureen is a different case entirely.' Tired as she was, she could not allow it to pass without a fight. 'Mary-Maureen was always a rough child. She was always getting over-excited and taking it out on the other children. There was violence in her from the beginning.'

'That's what I mean – ' Vera closed in eagerly to make her point. 'She should have been put away as soon as she got too big to control. It was her parents' fault, as much as hers. Letting her roam around free and play with the children in the neighbourhood, as though she were a child herself. Of course children play rough and get over-excited – and push. It's lucky the lights had been red and the cars hadn't had time to get up any speed when she pushed that little girl into the traffic. Both her legs broken, wasn't it?'

'That's right.' She tried to leave it there, but Vera wouldn't have it.

'Well, then.' Vera nodded sagely. 'It just goes to show, doesn't it?'

'To show what?' She faced Vera squarely – she'd make her *say* it, and enough of this pussyfooting around.

'You ought to think of Sheila more.' Vera backed off and attacked on the flank. 'She's getting on. Twenty-five, isn't it? And not married. Nor likely to be, with Denny hanging about where any boys could see him when they came to call. It puts them off – to see someone like that in a girl's family.'

'Denny *is* a part of the family. Sheila has always accepted that.'

'We're not talking about what Sheila accepts, we're talking about what a *man* will accept. You're ruining her chances.'

'Sheila would never marry a man under false pretences, anyway. If Denny weren't there, she'd tell the man about him. So it doesn't make any difference. You should know that.'

Vera's exasperated sigh said that she did, that she didn't know why she didn't wash her hands of the whole lot of them and stop giving good advice that wasn't appreciated. But they were her family, so she was driven to persist.

'That may be all very well for now, but you're not getting any younger, you know.'

'Neither are you, Vera.' She couldn't resist that one.

'Just what I mean. And Denny's what? Thirty? He'll outlast us all. Poor Sheila will be saddled with him till her dying day – and he'll probably outlast her, too. God help us, but it would have been better if it had gone the other way around.'

She'd thought of that, too, God forgive her. It wouldn't have mattered quite so much if Sheila had been the one lacking. Denny, being the older, could have got a good job and been able to look after her. Sheila could have kept house for him, done simple cooking and – What was the use of thinking about it? It hadn't happened that way, and that was all there was to it. No, not quite all –

'You've been lucky, so far,' Vera said. 'Suppose Denny changed?'

'Why should he change?' She was instantly defensive.

'Ah, they can, you know, as they grow older.' Vera nodded, pleased at having got past her guard. 'They all thought Mary-Maureen was harmless, didn't they? And look what happened.'

'Denny is as gentle as a lamb. There's no harm in him. He wouldn't hurt a fly.'

'Maybe not – while you're here to look after him. But what of when you're not here? When Sheila has to bear the burden on her own?'

What of it? There was a whole bottle full of the pills she had so painfully saved. And she'd get another whole bottle of them tonight. *Sheila would understand.* She closed her eyes against a twist of pain.

'You needn't worry, Vera,' she said coldly. 'I'll take care of Denny. I'll always take care of Denny.'

DENNY

Rembrandt didn't see him coming. Denny tiptoed from the corner, to surprise him. Just as he got there, Rembrandt began searching through his box of chalks for the right colour to finish off his cocker spaniel penny-catcher.

With a crow of triumph, Denny swooped on the box, snatching up the tawny gold chalk and offering it to Rembrandt.

'No.' Rembrandt shook his head, stepping back out of Denny's shadow. 'You found the chalk, young-fellow-me-lad, you can finish the picture.'

Denny promptly crouched on the pavement, tongue clenched between his teeth in concentration. He had been allowed to do this before, when Rembrandt was in a good mood. And sometimes he had done nearly a whole picture all by himself. This time, though, the cocker spaniel was almost finished. There was just the soft curly ear to fill in, and the highlights. Denny worked at it in the light feathery strokes he had watched Rembrandt use.

'Good. Very good.' Rembrandt stood looking over his shoulder. 'You'll be taking over my pitch before I know it, if I don't keep my eye on you, young fellow.'

'I wouldn't do that,' Denny said, glancing up at him. It was funny, the way Rembrandt always kept calling him 'young fellow', because Rembrandt must be about the same age. He looked the same – about the same height and weight, about the same number of funny wrinkles around his eyes when he laughed. Yet, in some way, Rembrandt *was* older.

The other lines in his face were in different places. Between his eyes and down the sides of his mouth when he wasn't smiling.

Denny's face was not marked in the same way. He knew because he had spent long hours in front of the mirror, charting the differences. His face didn't have many lines. There were only the deep horizontal furrows of perplexity across his forehead, from trying to think things out.

Like now. Like wondering why he and Rembrandt should be so alike in size, and yet so different. They were both big boys; and yet, Rembrandt was bigger, older, in some indefinite way. A lot of really big boys were.

Denny stopped drawing, his mouth fell open slightly. He was conscious of a faint buzzing sound in his ears and the vague dizziness that beset him when he tried to plumb the depths of some problem. It was always about this time that his mother would say, *'Don't bother your head about it, Denny.'*

'Now, it can't be *that* bad, young fellow.' Rembrandt bent down and detached the chalk from Denny's fingers, finishing the drawing in swift neat strokes. 'Nothing ever is, when you can talk it over with a friend. What's the trouble?'

Denny shook his head. He'd tried to talk about it sometimes, with other people, but they'd just acted funny and looked away. Sometimes they walked away.

But Rembrandt was his friend. He couldn't explain what he meant, though.

'I'm not like you,' Denny blurted out.

'Oh, I see.' Rembrandt looked as though he really did see. 'No, you're not, Denny. And that's a fact.'

'Why?'

'Oh, Denny, my lad – ' Rembrandt sat on the pavement beside him – 'if I could answer that – '

Rembrandt looked sad, with something of the sadness that was in Mum's face sometimes. Denny wriggled miserably. He had said the wrong thing again, and he hated making people unhappy.

'God's will be done?' Hesitantly, Denny proffered the words he had heard priests say to his mother. Sometimes they comforted her, sometimes she cried later. (But big boys don't cry.)

'Denny, Denny,' Rembrandt sighed deeply, 'what kind of God do we worship? What Deity can demand so much and give so little?'

Rembrandt was sadder than ever. It hadn't been the right thing to say, after all. Denny opened his airline bag and rummaged inside, pulling out the packet of sandwiches.

'Lunch?' he offered. There was plenty for both of them, and he wanted to share it with Rembrandt. Rembrandt never seemed to have sandwiches of his own, and just went into a snack bar when he had enough money collected. On bad days, Denny suspected, he didn't eat at all. But this was a good day.

'No, thanks, Denny.' Rembrandt pushed the sandwiches away. 'I can't eat your lunch.'

'There's lots,' Denny insisted. 'I'm not very hungry.'

'And you think I am?' Rembrandt smiled wryly. 'You're wise in your own way, aren't you, Denny? Sometimes I think you might turn out wiser than all of us.'

'No,' Denny said, with finality. Something in him knew better than that.

'No,' Rembrandt agreed, with another sigh. 'It isn't that easy, is it? We can't stand back and salve our consciences that way.'

'Here.' Sensing he had won, Denny took one of the sandwiches out of the packet and thrust it into Rembrandt's hand. This time, Rembrandt did not resist.

'All right, Denny, thank you. I'll pay you back some day, when I'm rich and famous. When I've stopped being the oldest student in the class, busking his way through art school.' He bit into the sandwich savagely. 'I'll not deny I'm hungry.'

'Lots of sandwiches,' Denny said. 'Have some more.' He would almost rather watch Rembrandt eat than eat himself.

' "Feed my lambs", eh, Denny, boy?' Rembrandt gave a short sharp laugh.

Lambs? It would be nice to feed lambs, to run and play and jump with them. But there were no lambs in the centre of the city. Rembrandt was all mixed up again.

'Ducks.' Gently, Denny set him straight. 'Going to feed the ducks and ducklings. Down by the river.'

MERELDA

Sitting on the river bank, she closed her eyes, letting the soft breeze from the river blow away the lingering memory of too much cigar smoke, too much port. The effort of repressing her distaste, her boredom, her sheer hatred of the whole proceedings, had exhausted her. She felt she could stretch out on the bank and sleep for days. But that would never do.

She concentrated on the only thought that was able to relax her lately. Her refreshment . . . and her obsession. The gun in Keith's desk drawer in the study.

The gun – he had no permit for it. He kept it in case of housebreaking, and because he occasionally had to travel in lonely districts carrying large sums of money.

The gun – he kept it loaded. ('Not as though we had to worry about children. No toddlers, who might get hold of it, eh, lass?' The implied criticism setting her teeth on edge. He had bought her, did he have to exact the last full pound of flesh, too? Did she have to give him a child? Once trapped with a child, she might never find her way back into her own world. One more reason for getting it over with quickly. The hints were growing broader, the impatience less veiled.)

The gun – a soft, dreamy smile curved her lips. Accidents were always happening with guns. Especially guns kept loaded.

Guns went off; people died. And, afterwards, a pretty widow with tears in her eyes would beg the police to take the gun away and keep it. She didn't want it in the house — she should have persuaded her husband to give it up years ago, in the last amnesty. She never wanted to see it again. A nice touch, that, and one the police would appreciate. It was genuine. Afterwards, she would have no further use for a gun.

Afterwards . . . a pretty young widow with plenty of money to finance an independent production could write her own terms in the film world. A script tailored to bring out all her best features. A light comedy, perhaps, to start. She could go into drama later. When her stardom was assured.

Afterwards . . .

First, the accident must . . . happen. In a way which would not involve her. Or involve her only in the most peripheral manner. An innocent bystander. Perhaps . . . a potential victim herself.

Guns went off when they were being cleaned. It was an idea, but not a very satisfactory one. He wasn't the sort to be careless about a firearm. About having one without a permit, yes. About handling it, caring for it, no.

Apart from which, it meant a direct confrontation. There was always the possibility of error. Of something going wrong. Of Keith, still alive, knowing what had been attempted, ready to accuse . . . to punish. That was unthinkable.

The best way was one which could be passed off as an accident, even to the victim, if it failed.

That meant there must be someone else there to take the blame. Preferably someone who would do the actual work. Someone who could be cajoled . . . or tricked . . . into pulling the trigger.

A catspaw.

The smile faded from her face, replaced by a frown. That wasn't so easy.

Not a friend of hers. There must be no hint of collusion. That ruled out acquaintances, too, to be on the safe side.

A stranger. Someone unknown as yet. Someone agree-
able . . . malleable . . . who could be introduced into the
house without exciting either jealousy or suspicion.

There was noise now from the river, an excited quacking
and splashing of ducks, the muted shouts of a child. The
noise grew, making it difficult for her to concentrate.

She opened her eyes and saw him.

He stood on the river bank, tossing fragments of bread
to the milling ducks. He was tall and good-looking and,
even as she observed that, the feeling came of something
being wrong about him.

Three ducklings squabbled suddenly, disputing a crust,
and he laughed aloud. His laugh was too abrupt, too
loud, too unguarded. It proclaimed an unsuspected vulner-
ability.

She realized now that she had been vaguely aware of
him before. He was often around this section of town, he
must live not too far away.

He turned and smiled at her trustingly, inviting her into
his enjoyment of the day, the ducks, the river.

A deep visceral shudder shook her uncontrollably, as
though she stood at the edge of an abyss looking down into
the hells that nature can create. His face was handsome, clean-shaven, amiable and . . . untenanted.

She drew a deep breath. After a long moment, she
smiled back deliberately.

DENNY

She was the prettiest lady he had ever seen. Her soft long
hair was the tawny golden colour of Rembrandt's pastel
chalk. Her eyes were bluey-greeny-grey – he couldn't decide
which. He stepped a little closer, trying to decide.

Her face had the soft warm radiance of the statues of
the Madonna in church. She smiled, and it was the
smile the Madonna sometimes seemed to give him as he
stared up at her through the shimmering heat haze rising

from the bank of lighted candles at her feet.

'Hello,' she said, still smiling. He looked around, but there was no one behind him. No one else there at all. She was talking to him.

(*'Don't speak to strangers.'*) His mother's voice echoed once in his ears and faded away, receding like the ripples on the river. This wasn't a stranger – this was the Fairy Queen in the Christmas Pantomime, the Madonna from her altar. And she was talking to *him*.

'Hello,' he said.

'Feeding the ducks?'

He wouldn't have answered a silly question like that for anyone else. They could see what he was doing. But she was different. She could ask anything she wanted to.

He nodded. She was smiling at him, as though she didn't know what to say next. He felt a momentary panic – she might go away. He wanted to keep her here, to look at her, to hear her voice again.

Maybe *she'd* like to feed the ducks, too. He pushed the crust he was holding at her.

'No. No, thank you.' She recoiled slightly. 'You go ahead.'

He looked down at the greasy, heavily-buttered, crumbling chunk of bread, seeing it momentarily through her eyes. If she took it, she might get her nice dress dirty.

Without turning, he threw the crust over his shoulder towards the barely-remembered ducks. Discarded, along with his afternoon's plans, along with anything else that might come between him and this pretty lady.

He wiped his hand along his trousers instinctively, holding it out to her so that she could see that it was clean. Not that he would ever touch her – his fingers curled away, as though he could already feel the soft silkiness of that shiny, beckoning tawny hair – Mum had warned him over and over again. (*'Never touch anyone, never try to.'* The strange sadness had been shadowing her face. *'People might misunderstand.'* Her face cleared as she added briskly, decisively. *'Big boys don't touch other people. You want to act like a big boy, don't you, Denny?'*)

Sometimes, big boys did. He had seen them, walking along by the river, with their arms around a girl's waist. He had laughed when he was smaller, joining the younger boys in jeering at this weakness they could not comprehend.

But now – Now –

Something teased at the corners of his consciousness, a tantalizing flicker of awareness of something beyond him – just out of reach. Something important. He stood absolutely still, frozen, as though – if he didn't move and frighten it away – he might catch it – learn some secret, find his way across some unknown boundary.

'Here.' She moved suddenly, rummaging in her handbag.

Diverted, he watched her, the train of thought so easily derailed sliding off its tracks again.

'Here,' she said, surfacing triumphantly with a wrapped sweet. 'Have a sweet.'

('*Never take sweets from strangers.*') His mother's warning rippled through his mind and eddied away. This wasn't a stranger. This was a pretty lady. Kind and friendly. He would have accepted the sweet from her had it been unwrapped – dirty, tacky and with crumbs of tobacco clinging to it, as were the sweets Rembrandt sometimes pulled from his pocket, which he took politely and threw away later – he would even have eaten hers.

He moved nearer, taking the sweet, but not withdrawing with it, towering over her, beaming down at her. She looked up at him and he felt suddenly that she did not like him standing over her. People didn't. Only Rembrandt never minded, but Rembrandt was as big as he was – maybe that was why.

'Do you live around here?'

Denny nodded. 'Over there.' He waved a hand vaguely in the direction of home, somewhere off in the distance.

'So do I.' She smiled, waving her hand in an opposite direction. 'Quite near here, really.' She hesitated. 'Would you like to come home and have tea with me?'

It was too much. Too sudden. He retreated slightly, hanging his head, unsure how to answer. He'd like to. More than anything. But – He retreated a bit farther.

'Don't be shy,' she coaxed, a hint of a frown clouding her face. 'We'll have lots of biscuits and nice cakes.'

He had displeased her, he knew. Now he stood staring dumbly, willing to do anything to bring back her smile, but powerless to retrieve the situation. His fists clenched and the sweet wrapper crackled in his hand. He unwrapped the sweet quickly and popped it into his mouth.

'Thank you,' he said around it, remembering belatedly that he had forgotten to say it at all. Perhaps that was what had annoyed her. He hadn't meant to be impolite, but it was hard to remember all the things he was supposed to do.

She was still looking at him in that strange, considering way. He wondered if he had done something else – or not done something. People got upset both ways.

'I've seen you around,' she said thoughtfully. 'I know . . . I've seen you at the church.'

'I've seen you there,' he said. He beamed. He *did* know her – she wasn't a stranger. 'Behind the candles.'

'That's right.' Her face changed slightly. 'We're . . . friends, then. Old friends. So . . . you can come to tea?'

'Yes,' he said blissfully.

She rose in a flowing graceful motion, her pale blue scarf floating from her fingers, and moved closer.

'Come along, then.' She took his arm.

Trustingly as a puppy, he went with her.

MERELDA

It was hard! Harder going than she had imagined it could be. How old was he? She glanced upwards at the dreamy face. Physically, anywhere between twenty and thirty. Who could tell with this sort?

Mentally? Four or five? Ten or eleven? Or did he slide back and forth? Older when he was faced with something he could understand; younger when he was out of his depth. Like all kids. But he wasn't a kid – not to look at,

although he was in every other way. What could she say
to him? How could she talk to him?

Still, she'd done all right, so far. It had been a bit
sticky until she'd mentioned church. She had suddenly
remembered seeing him coming down those steep stone
steps, clutching that same airline bag. (Or had she remembered it before – long before – and unconsciously been
searching him out?)

But what did he mean about seeing *her* in church? And
what was that crack about 'behind the candles' supposed
to mean?

'My name is Denny,' he said. 'Dennis. But everybody
says Denny.'

He wanted conversation. She had let herself in for this,
though, she had to go along with it. She'd just have to try
to meet him on his own level . . . if only she could discover
what that level was.

'My name is Merelda,' she said, equally confiding.
'Esmerelda, really, but everybody calls me Merelda.'

She had insisted on it. Dropping the 'Es' as soon as
possible, hating the background of it, knowing her mother
had seen some cheap film during pregnancy and thought
the name romantic. It wasn't so bad with the front of it
clipped off – she was able to feel it was vaguely 'U'. And
it saved being called 'Essie'. No one quite knew what to do
with 'Merelda'; she wasn't the type to be called 'Merry'.

'You must call me Merelda . . . Denny.'

'Merelda – ' He tried the name cautiously, rolling it,
tasting it. It was a nice name. He liked nice rolling names.
'Like Rembrandt'.

What was he on about now? No matter. Get him into
the house, let him see the layout of the place, and then
she could shove some tea into him. He couldn't talk while
he was eating. At least, she hoped he wouldn't try. Meanwhile, agree with him . . . humour him.

'That's right,' she said. 'That's exactly right. How
clever of you to notice it.' (Whatever *it* was.)

He gave a little skip. 'Merelda,' he said again.

Three years old? If only she knew more about kids. She never thought she'd feel the lack, but now she wished she'd paid more attention to Melody's brats on the rare occasions when she'd visited them. (Her sister, 'Melody' – relict of another cheap film seen somewhere in a hazy and senti- mentalized parental past.)

'Do *you* know Rembrandt?' he asked.

'*Everyone* knows Rembrandt,' she said firmly. She watched him nod happily. At least, *that* had been the right answer. She wondered if she should say anything more about art and artists . . . not that she knew much more. Did he? . . . *Could* he? What strange pockets of knowledge were hidden in that vague shapeless intellect? Better not take the conversation any further. Let him go on . . . if he wanted to.

'We're nearly there,' she said with relief, quickening her steps. Then shuddered, as he lengthened his own stride effortlessly to keep pace with her. There was a frightening amount of strength leashed within that mindless body. If it came to it, she would be powerless to outrun him . . . out- fight him.

If it came to what? She shrugged, throwing off the vague uneasiness. She was in complete control of the situation – a sideways glance at Denny, trotting docilely beside her, reassured her of that. He was so childlike a slap on the wrist, and a 'naughty' would bring him to heel, as it did any of Melody's brats when they got stroppy.

'Here we are.' She led the way up the steps and into the shadowy hall. 'We'll go upstairs, it's nicer there.' Up to the first-floor double drawing-room, with the immense picture window framing the constantly changing panorama of the river.

'Oh, first.' She paused, as though the thought had just come to her. 'Would you like to leave your things in here?' She opened the door to Keith's study, smiling, and motioned Denny inside. He moved obediently towards her, clutching the airline bag a little tighter, but prepared to part with his coat.

So far, so good. She watched him shrug out of his open

coat, fold it neatly and lay it across the couch in the corner of the room.

But Denny must not only know the layout of the house, he must be seen to know the layout. She rang the bell for the maid.

Ethel was there so quickly it was obvious that she had been lurking outside, trying to catch a glimpse of the male stranger Madam had been bold enough to bring into the house in the master's absence. Well, let her take a good look.

'We'd like tea, please, Ethel,' she said smoothly. 'Upstairs, I think. The view is better. And, Ethel, we want lots and lots of sweet biscuits, and buns, and jam, and cakes. Don't we, Denny?'

He turned from the couch, with his serene and vacant smile, to nod. She heard Ethel's sharply indrawn breath, felt the instinctive shrinking away momentarily that every woman must have at this threat. This positive reminder of what 'happily ever after' could really turn out to be.

'Oh yes, madam. I'll see to it immediately.'

As Ethel hurriedly left the room, Merelda caught the backward glance at both of them. The glance that told her she had made her play successfully. The awe – almost adoration – directed at herself; the primitive fear lashing out at the unrealizing Denny. ('Oh, yes, your worship. Madam was ever so kind to him. Brought him into the house and treated him just the same as you or me. When I think of what he's done . . . to repay her . . .') Floods of tears should complete the scene, although Merelda wasn't sure that they actually would. Servants weren't what they used to be.

There was one other thing, now.

'Denny.' Casually, she slid open the desk drawer. 'Have you ever seen a gun, Denny? A real gun?'

POLLY

The afternoon would never end. The seconds-hand of the electric clock swept smoothly and inexorably around the dial, but the other hands never seemed to move at all. Hours yet, before she went off duty. Hours yet, before she could go to the doctor and get the prescription; go to the chemist and have it filled. Hours yet, before –

The swish of rubber tyres approached along the corridor. Mustn't be caught napping. She opened her eyes to see the volunteer worker pushing the trolley of library books towards her. She forced a smile and stepped aside, so that the volunteer could wheel the trolley into the ward.

Then she leaned against the wall, closing her eyes for a moment. Perhaps, when she opened them, the hands of the clock would have moved a bit farther on. Just far enough to show that it was working, that this afternoon would end some time.

As it was, she seemed already trapped in eternity, existing in some quiet grey corridor of purgatory. Ah, but she wasn't going to purgatory. Not for what she was about to do. Let there be no presumption, no false hope. She'd be doomed to –

'Why don't you go home early, if you're not feeling well?' Vera was there in front of her, sharp little nose twitching, as though she scented brimstone. 'That's the sensible thing to do. No need to make a martyr of yourself, dragging along when you can barely stand.'

'I'm all right.' Sheer stubbornness stiffened her backbone, held her upright. It was fatal to show any weakness to Vera; besides, she wouldn't give her the satisfaction.

'You don't look it,' Vera said briskly. 'You look worse than you did at lunchtime – and that was bad enough, God knows. Why don't you go home now?'

'I'm all right!' She snapped it out in fury, feeling the false colour mount into her face, giving her the semblance

of health she had not had in some time now. 'Please leave
me be. There's nothing wrong with me.'

'Oh no,' Vera mocked caustically. 'You're fit as a fiddle,
we can all see that. That's why you're nearly fainting
every time there's a loud noise anywhere near you. And
why you're like to fall over if a strong wind's blowing.'

'I'm all right.' Like eternity, the phrase was endlessly
with her, all she could say. Her only defence.

'All right,' Vera said. 'Have it your way. At least, come
and have some tea. Come along now, it will do you good.
At least,' her voice wavered doubtfully, 'it won't do you
any harm.'

There was no use arguing. Polly allowed herself to be led
along the tiled corridor, although her throat had closed up
protestingly at the mere thought of trying to force anything down it. Vera was not to be denied. It was better
to give in to her on a small point like this before she
forced acceptance of some larger, more important, point –
like going home. The next step would be offering to go
home with her, to see that she got there safely.

'I'll take you home, if you like,' Vera said. 'They can
spare me for an hour or so. Just to see you settled in bed
with a cup of tea and a hot-water bottle. The weather is
treacherous, this time of year, and you need to be kept
warm and comfortable – '

'I'm all right,' Polly ground out again, between clenched
teeth. *Just leave me alone*, her whole being, her whole
attitude shrieked.

'Well, I don't know – ' She could feel Vera's doubtful
eyes on her. Vera had received the message but, it being
unspoken, had denied it. (*'Unless I see the wounds with my
own eyes, unless I put my hand into His side – '* There was
good precedent for the Veras of this world.)

They had reached the canteen and, with the prospect
of something practical to be done, Vera's indecisiveness
vanished. 'You go and sit down,' she said. 'I'll get the tea.'

Easier to obey than to argue. Polly instinctively made for
the darkest corner. The less light, the less Vera could
inspect her, those prying, glittering eyes raking every vein

and wrinkle for some clue to the cataclysm happening beneath the surface. She sat in the shadows, her back to the wall, fittingly enough. Vera always made people feel that they had their backs to the wall. What would Vera do if, suddenly, one of these cornered people decided to fight?

'There now . . .' She hadn't been aware that she had closed her eyes again until she opened them to focus on the tray Vera set in front of her with a small slam of satisfaction. 'You just eat this, and you'll feel better.'

By an effort, she kept her eyes open, but her throat closed up against the array of starches on the tray. 'Just a cup of tea is all I want.'

'Nonsense!' Vera buttered a slice of bread for her, as though she were a child, and thrust it at her. She took it automatically, setting it on the plate before her. She could manage a cup of tea, wanted one now, but the effort was all too much for her. She must save every bit of strength for the final effort tonight. After that, there'd be no more need to do anything. Ever. She waited, helplessly, for Vera to pour out the tea, which came in individual pots during the off-peak canteen hours.

From a great distance, she watched Vera fuss with milk and sugar, teapots and cups, saucers and spoons. A pity Vera had no children of her own to fuss over. It was all right now, while she had the hospital and the patients, but you could see it coming. The day when Vera, retired and living alone, would become the spinster scourge of her neighbourhood. The first one up in the morning to get to six o'clock Mass, and the rest of the day spent twitching aside the curtain at every faint noise of the local children, making life hell on earth for the rest of her neighbours.

But she wouldn't be here to see that. What did it matter to her, the way Vera might be heading?

Or would she see, from wherever she might? Might she be the cause of it? Partly. The reason Vera rushed out to pray at morning Mass, to light candles, to make endless Novenas? The reason Vera would watch the neighbours with jealous eyes, always seeking for some worse sin to measure the family disgrace against. Something unthink-

able, unmentionable, that might lessen the sin marked
against her sister-in-law's name for all the world to see.

As though there were worse sins than suicide. And
murder.

DENNY

'Gun,' Denny said. They were upstairs now, in the large
drawing-room overlooking the river, but the usually fas-
cinating river traffic was somehow less compelling than the
thought of the smooth, heavy object in the desk drawer
downstairs.

'That's right.' His nice new friend, Merelda, was smiling
broadly at him. 'In the desk drawer. We always keep it
there. Do you know anything about guns, Denny?'

' 'Course I do.' Did she think he'd never been to any
films, never watched television? 'You pull the trigger,' he
expanded. 'It goes bang. People fall down.'

'That's right,' she said again. He had the feeling that he
had pleased her greatly. 'And *why* do they want the other
people to fall down, Denny? Do you know *why* people shoot
other people?'

Why? His brow wrinkled in perplexity. Questions with
why in them were always the most difficult to answer.
They'd been talking so well. He hadn't expected Merelda to
start asking questions. Especially not questions with *why* in
them. He tried to think.

'Don't like them?' he suggested hopefully.

'Well . . . yes.' She frowned faintly, and he knew he
was losing ground. 'But . . . there's usually another reason.
The reason *why* they dislike them . . . isn't there, Denny?'

He nodded eagerly, still hopeful. Maybe she was going to
tell him.

She was. 'Because they're bad men, isn't that so, Denny?'
He nodded again, relaxing, as she went on.

'Because they're going to hurt other people – women
or children – and they want to save them. You wouldn't

stand by and let someone hurt a lady, would you, Denny? You wouldn't let someone hurt . . . me?'

'No!' It was impolite to shout, and he found he was on his feet with his fists clenched. He slumped back into his chair, lost in confusion, groping for words of apology.

But Merelda didn't seem to mind. She seemed pleased, even. Her smile was warmer than before. 'I knew I could depend on *you*, Denny,' she said.

He felt the warm flush rise into his face and twisted his head away. 'Nobody would hurt you,' he said. 'You're too pretty.'

Then there was a long silence. When he could stand it no longer, he swivelled his head shyly to see how she was taking it. Mum said grown-ups never made personal remarks. But he'd forgotten. And she was such a pretty lady.

'Oh, Denny,' she sighed. 'I wish you were right.' A sad little smile curled her mouth wistfully. 'But all men don't think the way you do. There's one – Oh, but I shouldn't bother you with my troubles. You came to tea. I want you to enjoy yourself. Have another cake, do.' She leaned forward, holding out the plate of cakes to him, but the ghost of sadness still haunted her lovely face.

'No!' Denny said, then realized she might think he was refusing the cake, and not refusing the thought that some wicked man might try to hurt her. He snatched a pink cake from the plate before she withdrew it. 'Thank you,' he said.

She seemed to understand. Her smile grew brighter, her eyes seemed larger and softer. She picked up the teapot. 'Have another cup of tea,' she said, in a voice like clotted cream.

Denny nodded dumbly, holding out his cup. Somewhere deep inside of him there must be some words to tell her what he was feeling, to assure her that he'd take care of her, protect her, as he'd protect Mum or Sheila, if danger threatened. But the words wouldn't come – they never came. He could only blurt out bits of what he felt.

'Nobody would hurt you. I wouldn't let them. I'd hit them. I'd – I'd shoot them!'

'Thank you, Denny,' she said, accepting the loyalty and the promise. 'If only . . .' she broke off and sighed.

'What?' he asked. 'Only what?'

'No . . . never mind.' She shook her head, smiling bravely. 'You can't be here when I really need help most . . . at night.'

Denny's heart lurched in wordless sympathy. He knew what she meant about night. He wasn't really afraid of the dark. Big boys aren't afraid of the dark. But night was a strange and dark time, with shadows moving in black corners, footsteps echoing down deserted streets, stopping abruptly and – when you looked out of the window, there was no one there, could never have been anyone there – strange cries and scuffling sounds at the end of blind alleys, shouts and fights when the pubs closed. Night was a bad time, full of bad things. Anything bad could happen in the night.

'But perhaps . . .' she said thoughtfully, 'perhaps . . .'

He leaned forward eagerly. Once again, she seemed to be offering him a solution to some strange question she hadn't quite asked, but which still hung in the air. 'Perhaps what?' he urged her on.

'Perhaps . . . if you could be here just *one* night . . . to frighten him. You're so big and strong – and bullies frighten easily. I expect you know that.'

Denny nodded. 'I've frightened them.' The gang of hooting boys, who had followed him through the streets some while ago – when? Last year? Year before? Longer than that? He rubbed his forehead. Time was like night and other things. Try to think about them too much and you grew dizzy and your head ached. ('*Don't bother your head about it, Denny.*')

'Once,' he said, 'once I scared them good.' They hadn't expected him to be waiting for them around that corner. They'd made his life a misery all day, following him around, jeering at him, throwing pebbles at him, scattering when he turned around, but re-forming into the pestering, gad-fly gang as soon as his back was to them again. And it was only the beginning of school holidays. ('*Ignore them,*

Denny, and they'll get tired and go away.') It was all very well, Mum talking like that, but it had never happened to her, and she couldn't really understand how it felt. She couldn't understand, either, that bad kids didn't get tired of teasing him as quickly as she thought they did. They came back, again and again. Just when you thought they'd gone off and found something else to do, they were behind you again, shouting and throwing things. You had to do more than just ignore them.

He had waited until late one afternoon. They were tiring of their game then, but had thought of nothing new to replace it. He'd led them out of their own familiar territory and got a bit ahead of them, and cut down an alley he knew about. They'd thought they'd lost him. It was beginning to grow dark and, watching from the shadows, he had seen the uneasiness growing in them as they realized how far from home they'd strayed. They'd huddled together briefly, some of their cockiness leaving them, and obviously decided to abandon the game of baiting Denny and go back to the comfortable familiarity of their own neighbourhood. Unsuspecting, they'd turned and begun retracing their steps.

He'd waited until they were almost upon him, then leaped out into the centre of the pavement, waving his arms and shouting, in his turn. He'd scared them, he'd really scared them good!

They'd wheeled and run, screaming for help. Pursued by his gyrating shadow, cast by the street lamp behind him, stretching out eight feet long, so that he'd only had to run after them a few yards to make them think he was going to chase them for ever. He'd had to laugh. When he was laughing so hard that he could no longer run, he stood there, his laughter booming out with the uncontrolled note that always made Mum say anxiously, *'All right, Denny, don't get so excited.'*

So, he'd stopped laughing, except softly to himself now and then on the way home. Those bad kids had run in the wrong direction – that was a good joke, too. He'd bet they got so lost it would be hours before they found their way back. He'd enjoyed that moment, really enjoyed it.

Only then, the police had come. '*A complaint*,' they'd
said, '*from the parents. About an incident.*' There had
been tears – Mum's mostly – and he'd tried to explain.
They'd seemed to understand. They'd let him off with a
warning, they'd said, but it must never happen again. Mum
had made him promise it wouldn't – no matter how much
the bad kids teased him. And it hadn't. Because the bad
kids hadn't come after him again. Just that once, he'd
fought them with their own weapons, and they'd never
bothered him again.

So, maybe Merelda was right when she said he'd only
need to scare her bad man once. Just once, and he'd be
good. And Mum need never know. And it wouldn't be the
same as scaring kids littler than himself, even if the police
found out about it. Although, with a rueful nod, Denny
acknowledged the truth, he was bigger than practically
everybody – except Rembrandt. Most grown-up men, he was
bigger than. Only, in some funny way, it never seemed to
make any difference.

And Mum would get awfully upset, if she ever found
out. So would Auntie Vera. '*The incident.*' That was the
way they still referred to that time, in hushed voices, when
they thought he wasn't paying any attention. And they'd
been talking about it again recently. It seemed to have
something to do with Mary-Maureen's getting sick and
going away for a long rest. That, too, had seemed to upset
the family.

Maybe it wasn't such a good idea of Merelda's, after
all. Maybe there was something else she could do that
would work better, and then he wouldn't have to break
any promises. He looked across the table at her.

'. . . Denny? Isn't that so, Denny?' She must have been
talking to him for some time, and he hadn't been paying
attention. She was biting her lip, the way Sheila did when
he wasn't being quick enough, smart enough.

'Yes,' he nodded eagerly, not sure what he was agreeing
to, but anxious to please her.

'Oh, I'm so glad you think so, too.' Her face cleared and

the smile he adored beamed out at him. 'It's always best to get things over with, once they've been decided on, isn't it, Denny?'

Uncertainly, Denny nodded again.

'Then, you'll do it soon, Denny. Very soon. You'll come back here, and let yourself into the house – the spare key is under the last flower-pot on the top step – and you'll . . . help me.

'But soon, Denny, very soon. I . . .' Her eyes filled with tears. 'I can't go on much longer. Tomorrow, Denny? Or . . . better still, if you could only manage it . . . tonight. Tonight, Denny?'

SHEILA

All right, face it, he wasn't going to call. He was never going to call again. He wasn't the first – undoubtedly, he wouldn't be the last. She ought to be used to it by this time.

She slammed the oven door shut, hurled the fork clattering into the sink, taking it out on the small inanimate objects around her. Because who else could you take it out on? It wasn't Denny's fault. It wasn't her fault. It wasn't Mum's fault – or Dad's. It was just the way things were – and she was stuck with them.

The family were all used to it by now. They'd had a long time to grow accustomed to it. It was strangers, acquaintances, newly-made friends meeting Denny for the first time, who reacted as though poor Denny were some sort of obstacle suddenly encountered in the middle of what should have been a smooth path. Poor Denny. He was a big hurdle for the uninitiated to take – few of them made it.

By this time, she should have stopped minding. The worst had been in her teens, when childhood friends were turning into prospective sweethearts. They'd all grown up together, all lived in the same neighbourhood, gone to the same convent school. They'd known about Denny all their lives – accepted him – accepted her – she'd never expected it to make any difference to them.

But suddenly, the difference was there. In their eyes as they looked at her, weighed her up, with new adult wariness. Just two of them in the family – and one of them wasn't 'right'. To their thinking, that made the odds fifty-fifty on any children she might bear. As though the cruel trick nature had played on Denny were some kind of latent gene, to be carried down, like haemophilia, through the female line. A man looked at her, and had a vision of himself looking down at his eldest son – and seeing another Denny,

And so, they drifted away, the boys she'd known all her life. After that, she'd heard the banns read in church, gone to their weddings as they'd married her friends, been bridesmaid a few times. And the protective shell had begun to grow around her. *'Always a bridesmaid –'*

Sheila stabbed viciously at the stubborn eye of a potato with the paring knife. Why had she ever thought it might be different?

Working in the city-centre, meeting new people who knew nothing of her home life or her background, she had begun to think there might be a chance, after all. At first. And then the new difficulties had begun. When friendships had begun to blossom, when it was time for ties to grow closer, when dates began to insist on escorting her home, the problem rose up again. What did one do about Denny? Rather, what did one say about him?

'By the way, my brother is a mental defective'? Or, 'Don't be surprised when you meet my brother – he isn't all there'? Perhaps, just simply, 'I have an eight-year-old brother – mentally, that is'?

Or did you play it the smart way? Let some man thoroughly entangle himself before springing it on him? Even then, when – and how – did you let him know? Did you wait until the last moment? At the church, perhaps, when you walked down the aisle on Denny's arm, to meet the man standing at the foot of the altar, to see him look past you at Denny's pleasant empty face? Denny, giving the bride away.

Well, Denny had given her away this time, all right. Two weeks ago, to be exact. Two weeks without a phone call, without a note. Another hopeful romance ended. She knew she was losing the courage to start many more. She was ready to give up – renounce the world. No, not a convent – Denny couldn't come, too. And what would happen to him, if anything happened to Mum? Mum, looking thinner, tireder, more drawn, every day.

That was something she did not want to have to face. Something she would, inevitably, have to face some day.

But not yet. She put the potatoes on to cook, began setting the table, pushing away thought with the domestic busynesses that needed attention. Time enough to think later. Time enough to face the worst when it actually happened.

Bad enough, what had happened recently. The two of them, strolling down the high street, laughing together, delicately balanced in that mood which might veer either way. Pleased with the show they'd seen, pleased with the meal they'd had, pleased with each other's reactions, the intangible intimacy gradually growing. And then –

Then – Denny. Denny, loping along, like an ungainly puppy, his face brightening when he saw her. Heading straight for her, purposefully for once, eager and trusting. So trusting. She could not deny him – small use to, anyway, when he was so obviously sure of his welcome.

He'd halted in front of them, eyeing her brightly, trustingly, waiting for her greeting. There'd been no help for it, none at all. Already the English face beside her was congealing slightly. Puzzled, but with a wary remoteness ready to set in, as it had, when she'd turned to him and said, 'I'd like you to meet Denny – my brother.'

And that had settled the question of how to break the news to that one. Settled the question of what his reaction would be. Oh, nice, quite nice. He'd bought them both ice-cream – and then she'd gone home with Denny. And stayed home ever since . . .

There were metallic scrabbling sounds suddenly, and the front door clicked. 'Is that you, Denny?' she called out.

No answer, but more shuffling, scuffling noises. She put down the tea towel and went into the front hall, ready to be stern. Denny had an amazing capacity for being 'followed' by stray dogs and cats. They'd had to put their foot down about this long since. But it was hard, since you couldn't really explain to him that he constituted enough of a problem for one household, without complicating it with animals which needed looking after, too.

Aunt Vera was in the hallway, trying to keep hold of Mum's arm and march her along to the kitchen. Mum was trying to pull free, but not having much success. Aunt Vera, as they all had good reason to know, was incredibly tenacious – especially when she was convinced that she was in the right.

'What's the matter?' Sheila went forward to meet them, her heart sinking. Mum was so pale. 'Is anything wrong?'

'Wrong enough!' Aunt Vera whirled on her triumphantly. 'Your mother collapsed at work just now. I've had to take time off and bring her home.'

'I never!' Polly protested, like a child, still trying to pull away. 'I just came over faint, for a minute, and closed my eyes. I was just dizzy, that's all.'

'And when you opened your eyes again, you were on the floor. You collapsed!' Vera accused. She turned the accusation on Sheila, as she came forward to help.

'Your mother's dead on her feet. Has been, for a long time now. You ought to help her more, a great big strapping girl like you – '

'Sheila's a good girl,' Polly said. 'She helps a lot, and she holds down a steady job, too.'

'So do you,' Vera said. 'It's too much for you, why don't you admit it? Oh, it wouldn't be, under ordinary circumstances – ' the accusation was back in her voice, in her eyes.

'It's the strain you've been under, all these years, it's not doing you any good. And you're getting older, it's bound to get worse – '

'Please, Aunt Vera – ' Sheila broke off, leaving it there. Anything she could add would only make Aunt Vera worse. You couldn't tell her straight out to shut up. Nor could you suggest that she wasn't doing anything to help the situation herself, with her nagging. That would only bring the injured sniff, the hurt look, and the fifteen-minute monologue about how hard Vera tried, but no one appreciated her efforts, some day they'd learn, and so on. In fact, Vera looked as though she might be going to launch out on that speech now, with as little provocation as she'd already had. Quickly, Sheila tried to forestall her.

'Here, Mum – ' Sheila managed to detach Vera and lead Polly into the parlour – 'lie down for a bit, and I'll bring you a cup of tea. Or would you rather go up to your room?'

'She couldn't make the stairs – the condition she's in,' Vera snapped.

'I'm all right,' Polly said stubbornly. 'I'll stay down here because – because I've got to go out to the doctor as soon as his surgery opens. The doctor will fix me up just fine. I'm overtired, that's all. He'll give me something to let me sleep.'

'You need more than that,' Vera diagnosed. 'That's only treating the symptom, and not the cause – and we all know it.'

Polly shook her head. 'Denny's a good boy,' she said automatically.

DENNY

Denny stood at the picture window, watching the river traffic without really seeing it, replete with tea, cakes, and a curious warm bursting feeling of satisfaction such as he had seldom known.

'You're so good,' a soft voice was saying, just below his ear level. 'So strong, and so clever. Oh, it's so good to know that I have someone I can depend on, at last.'

Denny's chest swelled with pride. He didn't quite dare to look down at Merelda. 'I'll fix him,' he promised. 'I'll scare him good.'

'Of course you will,' she said. 'And with the gun, too. That will scare him more than anything. You *do* remember where the gun is kept, don't you?'

'In the desk downstairs.' It was a question Denny could answer easily. 'In the drawer.'

'That's right.' She breathed a sigh of relief. 'And I'll leave the key for you . . .?'

'Underneath the flower-pot.' He could answer that easily, too. 'On the top step.' For the first time, he felt grown-up, clever. He knew the answers to the questions Merelda asked him. He could do what Merelda wanted, he could protect her, look after her, make the bully stop hurting her. And Merelda would be his friend for ever. He had been right, earlier, it was a good day. It was a wonderful day. He had made a new friend. He had met Merelda – and the world would never be quite the same again.

'I'm so glad I met you.' She seemed to move faintly closer. 'Just today – it feels as though I've known you so much longer.'

That was the way Denny felt, too. He dared to look down at her now, his arm ached to slip around her, but he controlled himself rigidly. (*'Stop that, Denny! Don't be so free with your hands. All people aren't like you, remember. You're a big boy now.'*)

'Yes,' he said fervently. 'Yes.' He looked away again. Maybe he could scare the bully really good. Scare him so much that he went away for ever. Then maybe Merelda could move in with him and Mum and Sheila, and they could all live happily ever after. A glimmering golden future of happiness shimmered like a mirage on the horizon of his consciousness. Surely, Mum and Sheila would love Merelda as he did, and they could have wonderful times together. Surely . . .

An icy gust of wind seemed to swirl through the room and lash against them. The door on the far side of the

room slammed and the iciness built up until it wouldn't be
surprising if some gigantic glacier moved across the width
of the drawing-room, crushing them in its wake. Denny
flinched, and felt the small withdrawing movement
Merelda made, although she didn't turn around either.

'So here you are,' the voice was harsh and glacial. 'I
thought you might be glad to see me. But I wouldn't
have come home so early, happen I knew you were enter-
taining. I wouldn't want to interrupt anything.'

'You're not interrupting,' Merelda said, in a small, uncertain voice. Denny knew instinctively that this was the
bully. This was the man who frightened Merelda, hurt
her.

'I – I'm glad you're here.' To his ears, it was unconvinc-
ing, but the man did not dispute her openly. He felt, rather
than saw, her turn to face into the room. To face the bully.

'Aren't you going to introduce me to your friend?' The
harsh northern voice grated on his ears. 'Or didn't you
intend that we should ever meet, eh?' There was menace,
vague but threatening, in the voice. Again, he knew that
Merelda was shrinking from it. He could not stand by and
allow her to be intimidated like this.

'Of course I want you to meet my friend.' Her hand
was a butterfly touch on his sleeve, turning him to face
into the room. 'This is my friend, Denny. Denny, this
is . . . my husband.'

Denny was used to seeing people's faces change as they
looked at him. The man's scowl vanished abruptly, leaving
a curious momentary blankness on his face before he
forced a reluctant smile.

'I'm sorry, lass,' he said awkwardly to Merelda. 'For
a minute, there, I thought – '

'Shake hands with Denny, dear,' Merelda instructed,
and he moved forward obediently, holding out his hand.

Denny glowered at him, might as well start the frightening now, show him someone wasn't scared of him. Taking
the offered hand, Denny deliberately squeezed it with full
strength and saw the other man conceal a wince.

'That's quite a grip you've got there,' he said. 'Still, I'm glad to meet you, lad.' He was still trying to smile.

'How do you do,' Denny said mechanically. He kept on glowering and, gradually, the other man's smile faded. That was better. But, bewilderingly, Denny felt a curious reluctance to continue trying to frighten him. The man looked kind. Was it possible that he was the bully Merelda had described?

Uncertainly, Denny glanced at Merelda. The hard coldness of her eyes left him in no doubt. This was the bully. This was the man he must frighten with the gun. Later. Not quite now. Later . . . tonight.

'Denny was just leaving.' As though to point up what he had just been thinking, Merelda spoke to her husband. 'We've had a lovely tea, with lots of cakes, but it's time for him to go now.'

Her butterfly touch was on Denny's arm again, urging him past the man, towards the stairs. Denny moved obediently. The man also turned and followed them down the stairs, as though reluctant to let Merelda out of his sight.

In the study, Denny groped in his airline bag for a moment, surfacing with the tawny-gold chalk, which he peeked at quickly. It *was* the exact same colour as Merelda's hair. Satisfying himself on this point, he struggled into his overcoat, not noticing that Merelda slipped something else into his airline bag while his back was turned.

She was smiling when he faced her, buttoning his coat, and the man was standing behind her, his hands on her shoulders. Threateningly – or protectively?

'Come again, Denny,' she smiled, holding out her hand. Behind her, the man frowned.

'Thank you.' Denny tried to remember his manners. 'It was a very nice tea. Good night.'

On the pavement again, he found he was still holding the chalk in his hand. Under the street lamp, he bent and quickly drew the outline of her hair, as he remembered it, on the bottom cement step. The soft tantalizing curls sprang from the chalk as though they had been imprisoned within it, waiting for the stroke of chalk against cement to bring them to life. The colour was perfect. It would never be the same to draw a cocker spaniel's ears again.

But the rest of her was fading from his memory. Although he could still see her face when he closed his eyes, he knew he would not be able to recapture it in the other coloured chalks. Not until he had seen her again and again, knew her better.

Meanwhile, it was past tea time and Sheila would start to worry. So would Mum, when she got home, if he was not there. Women got upset about nothing at all.

He moved off in the direction of home.

POLLY

With Vera gone, the silence became a warm and cosy thing. The tiny, homely sounds from the kitchen, where Sheila was preparing tea, were reassuring in their eternal familiarity. (*As it was in the beginning, is now, and ever shall be –* ' No! That was blasphemy. A sin, another sin, among so many. And minor, when measured against –)

Polly sat up abruptly, swung her legs to the floor and sat on the edge of the couch until the dizziness abated.

'Mum, are you all right?' Hearing the springs creak, Sheila had rushed to the doorway.

'Yes, fine.' Polly blinked hard, blinked again, and the blur in the doorway became the slim silhouette of her daughter. 'I was just thinking it was time I was getting along to the surgery. Get there early, get home early – ' Her voice trailed off. Good job Sheila couldn't follow her thought.

'Are you sure you'll be all right? Wouldn't you rather wait until Denny gets home? Then I could go with you.' Sheila glanced at her watch. 'He's late. He should have been home half an hour ago. It *is* bad of him to be so late when you're not well. He knows you worry – '

'Denny's a good boy,' Polly defended automatically. 'He loses track of the time, that is all. God knows, it's not as though he could help it.'

'I suppose not,' Sheila said. Still, there are times when he could *try* harder. I'll – '

'Leave him alone!' Polly spoke more sharply than she had intended. 'I'll see to Denny!' She tried to soften her voice, to allay the uneasiness which had suddenly shaken Sheila. 'You just leave him to me.'

'It's marvellous,' Sheila agreed, 'the way he listens to you. You seem to make him understand when no one else – ' She broke off, as though there were thoughts of her own she didn't want anyone else following.

'Perhaps I can come with you, anyway,' she said. 'Surely Denny can manage for himself for one night.'

'No!' Polly said. Poor Denny, coming home to darkness, to an empty house, not knowing where everyone had gone – that was what she wanted to spare him. A lifetime of uncertain emptiness like that. For the time that was left to him, Denny must have the warmth and security he had always known.

In the kitchen, the kettle began to boil loudly. Sheila half-turned, but still hesitated in the doorway.

'Go and turn the kettle off,' Polly ordered. 'And stop fussing so much. I'm all right.'

After another moment, Sheila disappeared and the kettle stopped humming abruptly.

It had to be done, and the best thing was to get it over with as quickly as possible. Thinking about it didn't do any good. The decision was made, the time was past for thinking, for praying.

Polly scuffed her feet into her shoes and stood up slowly, the way she had learned to these past few months, so that the dizziness didn't overcome, or the pain rocket through her. Slowly, that was the way to take it. Slowly and unthinkingly, from this point onwards.

'I'll be going along now,' she called out, keeping her voice steady. Above all, she must act natural, seem the same as she had always been, so that nobody could suspect – until it was too late to make any difference.

'Are you sure you should?' Sheila appeared in the

doorway again, staring at her uncertainly. Polly smiled and straightened slowly.

'I'll be there early – get away early. That'll be best. Collect my prescription on the way home. Then I can take my pill, have a hot drink, and get to bed early.' Her smile wavered, steadied. 'Sure, I'll be a new woman in the morning.'

There was no poignancy about it being the last – or next-to-last – walk through the old neighbourhood. With detachment, Polly noted the changes of the years – almost unnoticed at the time they happened. Perhaps it was because of the feeling of being not quite present. Of already being half-way 'there' – wherever there was.

In the early days, she'd walked down this street often with Brian. In some funny way, he seemed to be close to her tonight. Or was it that she was closer to him? If so, she must cling to this feeling – because it would be all she had of him. For ever more. She wouldn't be with him after this, couldn't go where he had gone. They wouldn't even bury her in consecrated ground. Denny, yes. But not her. And yet, there was no other way.

(*No other way, Brian.* Her mind raced wildly, talking to him, trying to dispel the disapproval she felt emanating from him. *If 'twas me had gone first, and you was left, wouldn't you be doing the same now? He's ours, Brian, and nobody but us to look after him. Such as he is, he's our responsibility. Mine, now. If I can't stay with him, then he'll have to come with me. There's no other way –*)

'Good evening, Mrs O'Magnon.' The black figure on the other side of the low wall moved forward.

'Good evening, Father Flaherty.' Polly halted reluctantly. The last person she ever wanted to see again, and there was no escape.

'I haven't seen you at church lately.'

Briefly, she considered lying, saying she'd been going to a different Mass, but there was no escape that way, either. The parish was dwindling. There weren't so many other Masses, or so many priests, either.

'I haven't been feeling awfully well, lately, Father,' she said. 'Besides,' she added mildly, 'it's not a sin any more to miss Mass once in a while, is it? Not if you aren't feeling well?'

'No, no.' The old priest shook his head regretfully. 'But we must remember that the operative phrase is "once in a while", not just because it's convenient for us. We mustn't presume to –'

He had begun gesturing with the hand holding his breviary, and the black book caught his eyes. Crammed, it was, with bits of paper. Once it had been a solid, satisfying line of defence, its orderly bulk marked only by holy cards and memorial cards. Now, it bristled with communications from the Hierarchy – new prayers, new translations, new changes in the ritual. Fresh marching orders every week, it seemed, and no way of knowing any more who was out of step and who wasn't.

'Ah, Mrs O'Magnon,' he sighed, abandoning the homilies, 'we've seen a lot of change, you and I.'

'Indeed, we have, Father,' she said. 'I was just thinking that, coming along.' She'd seen the tell-tale glance at the breviary and followed his mind without effort. She'd known him long enough – he'd married her and Brian when he was a new curate; tried to comfort her, first over Denny, then over Brian's death. He was interwoven into the fabric of her life, and she into his. Like it or not, that was the way of it. And what she intended to do would come as a crushing blow to him. More so than to Sheila, perhaps. He was older and not so resilient.

'Everything's changing so fast,' he said fretfully. 'Look at that –' he waved his breviary at the new block going up across the street, where once a terrace of Victorian working men's cottages had stood. 'Are people going to live any better in vertical glass hutches than they did in the old houses? New places, new ways – that's all people think about nowadays. But are all the changes for the best?'

'I think most of them must be,' she spoke slowly, trying to choose the right words to absolve him of any sense of guilt at failing her when he looked back at the scene in the light of the knowledge he would soon have. He must not blame himself that he could not have read her mind and averted her from her planned course.

'Isn't it better that people should have the light?'

'Ah,' he pounced, 'but do they *see* The Light?'

'Isn't the whole point of it,' she said, 'that there are many lights? Aren't we now admitting that every man must be free to see his own? To follow the dictates of his own conscience, and not just dictates?'

'I know, I know,' he said. 'The curates keep telling me – '

She was contrite. He was old and tired. There were too many changes, happening too fast, for him. Perhaps for them all. It wasn't the church they used to know, and it was still changing. Could anyone blame the parishioners who had drifted away, deciding, *'We'll come back when you've made your minds up'*?

So many things were no longer strictly right or strictly wrong. There were still rules left, of course, but for how long? Perhaps, some day, even what she was about to do would be permitted – the law of the land had already changed about that. In a few more months, a few more years, who knew?

But she didn't have a few more years, nor even months. Her time was ticking away by the minute. It could be measured in hours now, the time left to her – and to Denny.

'I beg your pardon, Father?' He had been speaking, saying something to her, and she had missed it.

'No matter, no matter.' He gestured impatiently, and an envelope bearing an official seal slipped from the pages of the breviary and slapped against the ground.

Automatically, she bent to retrieve it for him and the pain caught at her middle. She gasped, and froze.

'Eh?' He picked up the envelope, brushing it off, and looked at her keenly, for the first time. 'You're not well, Polly O'Magnon. What is it?'

'Nothing, Father,' she denied quickly. 'Nothing serious. Sure, I was just on my way to the doctor now for some of the medicine to put me straight. I'll be all right.'

'And I've been keeping you standing here talking. I've

been selfish. Go along, I won't keep you any longer.'

'Yes, Father, I will then,' she said. 'It's all right, but I would like to get to the surgery before it gets too crowded.'

'Of course you would,' he said.

She started to turn away, when he called her suddenly. 'Polly – '

She turned back.

'God bless you.'

SHEILA

Mum had gone. Sheila sighed and put the chops in the pan. As soon as Denny came in, she'd turn the grill on. He'd be famished. He must have roamed a fair piece to be this late getting home.

That was another of the endless worries. Denny, roaming all over the city, into neighbourhoods where he wasn't known, where people might be alarmed by him, not realizing he was harmless. Where they might say or do something to upset him or hurt him.

But what could you do? You couldn't chain him up, the way they sometimes did in Victorian times. He was healthy and happy, he needed lots of fresh air and exercise. It was a perpetual question – one that came into the foreground every time Aunt Vera visited, with her pursed lips and her head-shaking and her endless hints about forebodings.

You could worry about everybody, though. There was danger in crossing a street. Anyone could be in the wrong place at the wrong time and be hit by a stray bullet, or a car out of control. Or – like Daddy – by a pile of building materials falling on him at a building site. Denny would just have to take his chances with the rest of humanity. It was a pity, though, that he wasn't so well equipped to deal with the things that might happen as the rest of humanity.

For that matter, it was time to worry more about Mum.

She was putting a brave face on it, but she wasn't getting any better. Although she denied it, she seemed to be getting worse. She'd never fainted at work before.

Perhaps it might be a good idea to drop in and talk to the doctor. Ask him if he'd really given Mum a thorough examination, or just taken her word for it that a few sleeping pills were all she needed. Ask him what was really wrong. Would he tell? Would he admit it – even to the next-of-kin – if Mum's illness was really serious? There was some medical rule, wasn't there, about doctors keeping their patients' secrets? Would that apply, in this case?

Don't worry, that was all doctors ever seemed to say. *Don't worry*. As though worry was something you could turn off, like the television set, by twisting a button.

Still, she ought to see the doctor, try to get an honest opinion out of him. In the morning, perhaps, she could telephone and let them know she'd be late to work, and stop in on her way to the office –

The front door slammed suddenly. 'Denny, is that you?' she called.

'It's me,' his voice agreed amiably from the front hall.

'Go and wash your hands, then.' She snapped on the grill. 'Tea's nearly ready.'

He clattered upstairs and was back again, in the briefest possible time, pulling out his chair and seating himself at the kitchen table. But he seemed in no hurry to start when she put his plate down before him and drew up the chair opposite.

'Aren't you hungry?' she asked.

He picked up his fork, more as though he wanted to show willing than to actually use it. 'Had some tea,' he said, 'with a friend.'

'That's nice.' Sheila was hungrier than she had realized. 'Anyone we know?' Denny was always on about his friends. Sometimes he meant stray dogs, or birds, and sometimes he meant people. It wasn't always easy to sort out his reports of his day. To be honest, she generally made listening noises and didn't really bother.

'Pretty lady,' Denny said. 'Lots of cakes.'

'That's nice.' Then something in his voice made her look up sharply. He was leaning forward on one elbow, idly building his mashed potato into a shape like a sand castle with his fork.

It wasn't like Denny to be uninterested in food, no matter how much he had eaten, or how recently. The strange, bemused expression on his face was new, too. Sheila felt a sudden pang. In somebody else, they might be symptoms of love – calf love, at least. But Denny? Denny?

Not another of Denny's crushes! They had been spared one for some time now, had been hoping that that phase might be over. Not that he was any great trouble. Like a child, he just wanted to follow the woman around, grateful for a few words, and he'd stand outside her house, just staring at it. Mind you, it often made the woman concerned very nervous (one had actually moved away because of it), and it added fuel to Aunt Vera's constant flaming concern. ('*It may be all right this time,*' she'd say darkly, '*but one of these days . . .*')

'What lady?' The sharpness of her voice surprised herself as much as Denny. It brought him sitting upright, injured innocence on his face. He'd done nothing to deserve that tone of voice. Nothing that he could remember, anyhow.

'Merelda,' he said, as though that explained everything. 'Merelda.'

'Merelda,' she tried to keep her tone quiet and even. 'Merelda – *who*? What's her last name?'

'I don't know,' Denny said cheerfully. 'Just Merelda. Pretty lady.'

'And where – ' she was calmer now, Denny looked like his old self again, she must have been imagining things – 'did you and Merelda go for tea and all those cakes?'

'Her house,' Denny said.

'And where – ' it was like sweeping water with a broom, you seemed to be getting somewhere and then you realized you'd made no progress at all – 'where is her house?'

'That way,' Denny gestured happily.

'Don't point! I'm sorry, Denny, I didn't mean to snap at you. Just tell me in words, can't you?'

'I don't know,' he mumbled. 'Along the river.' He was turning sulky now. He sat there, hunched up, and stabbed at his chop, pretending to concentrate on his food. She'd get no more out of him now.

Well, what did it matter? He was good-natured, but you could only push him just so far. Let him be now. So, some woman had taken him in and fed him like a stray cat – it probably wouldn't happen again. If it did, then she could find out more about the woman. Probably the woman had just been acting on a random impulse – it had happened sometimes when Denny was a little boy – and it would never be repeated. It would be too bad, though, if Denny built it up to more than face value somewhere in the mazes of his cloudy child's mind. But that was another risk you couldn't protect him from, another area where he had to take his chances with the rest of us.

Unconsciously, Sheila sighed. Denny looked up quickly, still defensive.

'It's all right, Denny,' she said quickly. She stood and moved to the stove, filling the teapot.

Denny ducked his head with relief. She turned in time to catch his other gesture.

'Use your handkerchief, Denny.'

Denny nodded, groping in his pocket. His hand connected with something greasy and unfamiliar. He pulled it out with his handkerchief. The remains of the buttered breakfast toast he had forgotten.

'What's that, Denny?' Sheila walked over to stand behind his chair, her hands on his shoulders, looking down at the greasy crumbs.

'Toast,' he admitted. 'To feed the ducks.' He looked up at her cautiously, waiting for the reprimand. 'I forgot it.'

'All right, I'm not going to scold you.' Sheila laughed abruptly, giving his shoulders a tiny shake. 'Oh, Denny, Denny, the tightrope you walk.'

Denny whirled suddenly and clutched her about the waist, his head burrowing for the sanctuary between her breasts. Like a child, responding to kindness like a child, but with a man's strong body.

She stiffened for a moment, then detached him gently and moved away. (*Oh, Denny, Denny, the tightrope we all walk.*)

MERELDA

'I don't like dafties!' He was a dark silhouette against the pale grey of the picture window. A bulky, menacing shape in the growing darkness.

'Nonsense, darling.' She touched a switch and the lamp glowed, giving him form and features again. 'Denny is harmless – and rather sweet, really.'

'Rather sweet! That's what you used to say about that other lot you always had hanging about.' His head jerked towards her, suddenly alarmed. 'Here! Now that we've got rid of that useless lot, you're not going to start filling the house up with his sort, are you?'

It was her house. She bit back the retort, forced her face into pleasant lines.

'There aren't *that* many around.' She kept a light, affectionate, teasing tone.

'And a good job, too.'

'You *are* being silly. He's just like a child. He was feeding the ducks and we started talking. He offered me – ' she laughed lightly – 'some of his bread, so that I could feed them, too. And then I thought I ought to offer him something – and I thought of tea. It was just an impulse. A sudden impulse.'

'You're too soft-hearted.' His face cleared and softened. 'You're too soft-hearted for your own good. That's the trouble with you, my lass.'

'Well, there's no harm in that, is there?'

'I'm not so sure. You don't want to encourage that poor creature to come hanging around you. You never know what they're thinking. Or what they might do.'

Yes, that was it. That was always it with men like Keith, perhaps with all men. That was why they saved the last bullet for their woman.

'That's . . . silly.' She let the hesitation and doubt creep into her voice, knowing that he would register them. At the same time, her mind couldn't help toying with the idea. How much of a man was there, controlled by that hazy, childish brain? What might it be like – that perfectly proportioned male body, directed – or undirected – by an unformed mind? Could he possibly – if goaded – ?'

'You're too trusting. And too impulsive. It can get you into real trouble some day. More trouble than you can handle.' He frowned. 'Perhaps more trouble than I can get you out of.'

'Impossible,' she said. He took it as a compliment.

'No, no,' he said, obviously flattered. 'I'll grant you, in the ordinary way, I could see you clear of almost anything. I reckon, perhaps, even murder. But that's when you're dealing with sensible people, who know which side their bread is buttered on. When you get someone like that – ' He broke off, the thought upsetting him more than he liked to show.

Someone like that. Someone to whom money, power and influence meant nothing, conveyed no threat and no promise. Were just words, as meaningless as the quacking of the ducks in the river.

She watched the half-formed thoughts flicker across his mind, reflected in his faint changes of expression, as clouds passing across the face of the moon cast their shadows on the earth beneath. He recognized Denny as a threat, but only as he felt a threat from anyone who might upset the ordered luxury of his way of life. He had no way of knowing how much of a threat Denny really was. She must keep him from finding out until the very last minute. Although . . . it would not do any harm to let him worry about Denny a bit more.

'I don't like dafties!' he summed up.

She suddenly wanted to shake his righteous arrogance. 'What's the matter?' she jeered delicately. 'Afraid of pre-natal influence?'

He went rigid with sudden shock, then his face lit up. 'Lass!' He crossed to her in a single stride and scooped her up into his arms. 'Lass, lass!'

She realized what she had said, then. She had meant *post*-natal, but her tongue had slipped, giving him something he had been waiting to hear since their wedding. Look at the way he was taking it – the room whirled as he swung her about in his arms – how could she recall that slip of the tongue now?'

'Lass, is it true? Is it true at last, then?'

'It won't be if you don't put me down and stop jarring me so.' That had been her chance – her only chance – to correct the mistake, and she had let it slide past, almost without realizing it. Too late now to go back.

'Sorry, sorry.' He set her down gently, she had suddenly become a piece of fragile porcelain. 'I just got carried away, like, for a minute.' His face was radiant.

Well, why not? A condemned man was entitled to a hearty meal. Why not let him have his dream? It wouldn't last long. Not long enough for him to do anything silly, like changing his will in favour of an unborn heir. Not even long enough for him to boast to any of his friends, so there'd be no need for the charade of a miscarriage . . . afterwards. (Although that wouldn't have been too much of a problem. No one would have been too surprised if an extravagantly grieving widow hadn't been able to carry a first child full-term. Or, if things took longer to work out than she planned, and Keith did get to a new will, it might even be possible to provide an infant heir. Not his – never his – but, possibly . . . Nick's.)

But that shouldn't have to happen. Things were working out quite nicely. Keith was going to be perfectly, blissfully, happy in his last hours – and she would have no unpleasant repercussions later. It was all very satisfactory.

'A son,' Keith was musing aloud. 'A son to carry on the business, to carry on my name. A son!'

'Don't be too sure.' Secure in her own magnanimity, she smiled up at him. 'It might be a daughter.'

'So much the better. Then I'll have two pretty little lassies to spoil – and we'll have a son next time.'

She repressed a shudder, seeing now what would have happened if she'd given in to him. What he really planned for her. One brat after another to inherit his precious industrial empire and carry it on. And what chance would she ever have had of breaking free of the nursery and getting back to the theatre? So much for his pillow promises of backing a production for her some time when she found something she really liked.

If there had ever been an indecision in her mind about the course she had embarked on, it was settled now. She was doing the right thing – it was self-defence, really. Not that a court might see it that way. But it would never come to a court. And, if it did, she would not be the prisoner in the dock.

'We'll have to be thinking of a good name,' Keith said abruptly.

'That's no problem,' she said. 'If it's a boy, he'll be Keith, Junior.' Really, it was amazing how smoothly she slid into the role; but it was an easy one to play.

'No –' Although he had set her down, he had not let her go. Now his arms tightened round her. 'No – do you really want to?'

'I wouldn't hear of anything else,' she said firmly.

'Young Keith.' He expelled a happy sigh. 'And if it's a girl, she'll be Little Merelda.'

'No!' Merelda reacted with complete honesty. 'No – I've always hated that name. I'd never inflict it on any child of mine!'

'All right, all right, lass, don't get so upset.' He patted her shoulder. 'Anything you say.'

'Perhaps . . . after your mother. I wouldn't mind that.'

'Aaah!' She had pleased him again. 'You're sure you wouldn't mind?'

'I just said so, didn't I?' She shrugged, speaking lightly. 'We'll use names for your family for – as the case may be – he, she . . . or it.'

'Don't talk like that!' he ordered, his arms tightening

around her again. 'Don't joke about a thing like that. It couldn't happen to us!'

'I'm sorry,' she smiled. 'Of course, it couldn't.' He didn't know what had already happened to them. Unimaginative and insensitive, he was only aware of the things that were thrust upon his consciousness. As Denny had been.

She realized now how fortunate she had been – although she had not thought so in those first moments – that he had come home early and discovered Denny. It gave him a focus for all his vague fears and forebodings. It directed his attention towards an intangible threat – and away from the real one.

'You'll promise me something now,' he said, still worried, 'and I'll give you anything you like. You won't let that creature come here again.'

'Oh, all right.' She gave in gracefully. 'Not if you don't want me to.'

'I don't. And if he comes, don't let him in.'

'But you're being rather silly about it. I don't believe he ever had any intention of coming again. In any case –' she laughed lightly – 'he probably could never find the way back here all by himself. Once he's away from here, he'll forget all about us.'

Even as Keith accepted this, she was suddenly petrified by the lie. Suppose it were the truth? Suppose, despite all her work and preparation, Denny put it out of his simple mind as soon as he was out of sight? How much, after all, could people like that retain of what they had been told? Could they remember what they had promised? And if he remembered, could he find the right house again?

Suppose he never came back? Tonight or any other night? She would be marooned with her deception on the shallow island of Keith's credulity. She would have to watch his trust gradually turn into puzzlement and then suspicion, as the months advanced with no visible sign of pregnancy. And Keith was not a man to trifle with – how many business associates had tasted the bitter proof of that fact? Keith was not a man to cross.

She shuddered slightly and tried to pull herself together.

There was nothing to do but go ahead with the evening as she had originally planned, counting on Denny not to get muddled about finding the house again. Counting on Denny to play his role, as she had outlined it, and not get muddled . . . until she intended that he should. In those final moments . . . Keith's final moments.

'What's the matter?' He had felt her shudder. 'Cold? Shall we have the fire lit?'

'Yes, would you, please?' It would force him to release her, move away from her. 'That's a lovely idea. It *is* a bit chilly tonight.'

Another good idea had been to tuck her blue scarf into a corner of Denny's airline bag. Remembering this, she relaxed slightly. In some odd way, she had felt this would be an additional motive for him to come back – even if he had forgotten the original motive. You could tell that he had been well brought up – the sort to be horrified to think he had walked away with someone else's property. He would come back to return the scarf and apologize . . . if for no other reason. And once he was here, she could take care of the rest of the situation.

'Penny for them, love.'

'I was just thinking,' she said slowly. 'Perhaps you're right. I wasn't entirely comfortable with poor Denny. Perhaps you noticed. That was why I didn't come over and kiss you when you came in. Somehow, I didn't want to . . . in front of him. I think I was afraid it might . . . give him ideas.'

'If he ever comes near this house again – ' Keith straightened up, the flames leaping into life in the fireplace behind him – 'I'll take care of him.' His face was dark, threatening. 'I don't like dafties!'

'Yes, darling,' she said softly, smiling with satisfaction. The stage was set . . . the trap was baited.

POLLY

After she had collected the prescription, she began to walk. Up one old familiar street and down another. She was not consciously saying goodbye to the neighbourhood where she had lived out her life. She had done that long ago – when the decision had first begun to crystallize. Now she was simply trying to delay her return home. Even though delay would change nothing, make no difference. Slowly and inexorably, the moment towards which she was moving would come.

Meanwhile, she walked. And Brian walked with her, in this last bitter while before the final, eternal separation.

(New curtains at the O'Haras – they've come up in the world, Brian. And the house painted last spring. Of course, all the four children have jobs now – they can afford to splash out a bit. Do you remember when Teresa O'Hara was in the bed next to mine in the maternity ward and I shared your flowers and chocolates with her because Pat couldn't afford any frills with two more at home? Our first, that was, our Denny – and we so happy, not knowing, never guessing, what he'd turn out to be. She had a son, too – an architect, he is, and moving up in the world all the time. Oh, Brian! The old pain stabbed at her with an intensity she had thought time had dulled. But it was here again, as fresh and hurtful as on the day they'd discovered the truth. Because she was so near the end and, in the end, you go back to the beginning. *Oh, Brian, why did it have to happen to us? What had we ever done? What were we being punished for?)*

'Are you all right, Mrs O'Magnon?'

People had been asking her that all day. Blinking away the tears, she saw the young policeman. Out of uniform now, but she recognized him, although she didn't know his name. She was vaguely surprised that he knew hers. But in a neighbourhood like this, everyone knew more about each other than it was comfortable to acknowledge. She was Denny's mother – that was why everyone knew her.

'I'm fine, thank you,' she said briskly. 'I'm just on my way home.' They both ignored the fact that she was wandering aimlessly in the wrong direction down a street that did not head towards her home.

'It's a nice evening.' He fell into step beside her. 'I'll walk along with you for a way, if you don't mind.'

'I don't mind.' But she did. With him here, Brian had withdrawn his faint and restless spirit, unable to compete with a corporeal presence at her side. And she had so little time left with Brian.

They turned into the High Street and Polly halted. 'Thank you,' she said firmly. 'I mustn't keep you any longer. I'll be all right now. I'm nearly home.'

He looked, for a moment, as though he would like to argue the point, then he smiled and saluted her. She walked away but, after a short hesitation, she heard the footsteps begin following her. Slowing when she slowed, stopping when she stopped.

He meant well. She felt a rush of annoyance. Everyone meant well, but none of them could understand. Why couldn't he go away? He was off duty, wasn't he? Why didn't everyone leave her alone to get on with what she must do?

But he was a policeman. Did policemen ever really go off duty? Did he suspect her? Know that she was about to commit a crime? The worst crime of all?

But, you see, Brian, I must. Slowly, she moved forward again. With the policeman behind her, she must go home now. It was time to go home, anyway. They'd have had their tea now, and Denny would be settled in front of the television until it was time for him to go to bed. Sheila would have done the dishes and, with a bit of luck, have gone off to visit one of her friends, or be sewing in her room. Safely out of the way.

The street lamps flickered on against the darkness as she turned the corner. A movement behind a lighted window caught her eye and she recognized the house.

Mary-Maureen lived there. Until they had to send her away. And that's part of the problem, too, Brian. Denny's so big now – and so old – he needs a man to control him. If anything should happen – if Vera's right in what she keeps thinking – what could we do? Two lone women. We can't watch over him every minute. Suppose he was to take a sudden fit of temper, like Mary-Maureen – although he's always been so sweet-natured? Sheila could never manage him by herself – and it would kill him to be sent away. He'd never understand. Oh, Brian, Brian, it's the only way –

Brian? She was alone, at her own gate, with her soul silently keening a name into the darkness. *Brian?* A meaningless word which no longer had the power to summon him to her side. Brian had gone on before her. A long way before – and there was no catching up with him. He was lost to her, as Denny would be lost to her. Both of them safe in the arms of the Lord in the afterlife. And she – she was already condemned. There was no turning back now.

She opened the gate and waved reassuringly to the constable, who stood at the corner, watching her. He made no move to leave, obviously he intended seeing that she got safely inside her own door. After that, if she collapsed, it was not his responsibility.

Carefully, now. She fitted the key into the lock, let herself into the house. *Act natural.* (Ah, God, could she even remember what was natural any more?) *Try! Very, very carefully – and very natural.*

'Mum, is that you?' Sheila – not gone out, nor even in her room, but hovering – waiting for her return. 'Are you all right?' She appeared in the doorway at the far end of the hall. 'What did the doctor say?'

'What does he ever say?' Polly hung up her coat. 'Get plenty of rest. Keep – ' Her voice broke. She took a deep breath and tried again – 'Keep taking those pills.'

A roar of canned laughter from the parlour and, over it, Denny's joyous chortle. Denny, God love him, watching his favourite programme. Such a good boy, Denny, and never a bother to her. Except in his own special way that he couldn't help.

'But – is that all?' Sheila looked strained and anxious. Could she have some premonition of the trouble in store? She'd never seemed so nervous and jumpy before.

'It's enough, isn't it?' Polly turned, still clinging to her handbag. (It weighed her down, the small bottle of capsules heavy as the weight of the world, as the weight of sin.) She could not put it down, afraid that it would topple over, spill out its deadly contents – and yet, there was nothing in it that should not be there. Sheila knew she was collecting a fresh prescription. In itself, it was perfectly innocent – nothing tell-tale about it. (It was only when you knew about the secret hoard of capsules hidden away upstairs that the deadly pattern began to form.) Still, she could not part with that handbag.

'I suppose so.' Sheila remained, irresolute, in the doorway. 'He didn't say how much longer you'll have to keep on taking them, or anything like that?'

'Not much longer,' Polly said firmly. If Sheila chose to believe that that had been the doctor's assurance, so much the better.

'Oh, good!' Sheila's face brightened. 'That must mean you're improving.'

'About time, isn't it?' Polly asked noncommittally.

'Yes – yes, that's the thing. It's taken so *much* time.'

'Everything takes longer than you'd think,' Polly said. (*Even dying? This final day had gone on for ever. She might already be in eternity – endlessly, limitlessly, it went on.* She felt a sudden icy chill. *Suppose that was what hell was all about? Not the searing eternal flames, but being trapped in time with your sin. Condemned to live the crucial day over and over again, feeling the grief and guilt as poignantly as if it were the first time. And it would be the first time, going on and on, repeating endlessly –*)

Polly swayed. 'I'm going upstairs,' she said abruptly.

'Do that,' Sheila said. 'I'll make you a cup of tea and bring it up. You can have an early night. It will do you good.'

'No!' *That wasn't careful, wasn't natural.* Poor Sheila was as startled by the vehemence of her retort as ever poor Denny could have been, wondering what she had said that was wrong.

'No,' Polly tried again, smiling. 'No, don't bother about me. I'll come down later and make cocoa for me and Denny. Why don't you go out for a while, now that I'm back to watch over Denny? Go to a film, or something. You stay in too much. It's not good for a young girl.'

'I'm all right.' Sheila was on the defensive now, as she always was when criticized about her social life – or lack of it. (Did she think her own mother didn't know the problem? Hadn't lived with it for longer than she had?)

'I'm not saying you're not. I'm only saying you ought to get out and about more. It's a fine evening, you ought to go for a walk, or something. Why don't you drop over and visit your Aunt Vera?'

Sheila looked startled, as well she might. (*Holy Mother of God – that was going too far. She'll be measuring me for a straitjacket, suggesting she go and drop in on Vera.*)

'You stay in too much,' Polly repeated. She watched, biting back compunction, as she saw Sheila begin to fear that she was in for a Vera-type lecture – if she stayed around.

'I could go down to the library,' Sheila offered placatingly. 'Are you through with your books? I could change them, as well as my own. And it would be a nice walk . . .'

She'd be gone about an hour and a half, if she did that. Would that be time enough? It wasn't long, but it was better than nothing.

'Do that, then,' Polly said. 'It will do for a start. You've got to think about getting out and about more. You don't want to spend all your days and nights tied to an ailing woman and a – a – And Denny.'

'I don't mind,' Sheila said quickly.

'But *I* mind!' Polly snapped. 'I mind very much. Remember that.' She softened her tone. 'I only want the best for you. I want you to be able to go out like other girls and – '

'I *am* able, I just – '

'I'm tired,' Polly said. 'Don't stand there arguing with me. Get along to the library and find me some nice books to read.'

'All right, Mum.' Sheila recognized the finality in her voice and turned away.

'Oh, and Sheila – ' Polly said casually. 'I may go to bed early, after all. If Denny and I aren't up when you get back, don't disturb us. An early night won't do him any harm, either.'

'All right, Mum,' Sheila said again.

Polly sat in the bedroom chair until she heard the front door close behind Sheila. Then she went to the window and watched Sheila walk down the path, saying the last goodbye that had to be a silent one.

You'll understand, Sheila. Perhaps not at first, but later. It's the best thing I can do for you. And for Denny. Perhaps, some day, you'll even forgive me.

After Sheila was out of sight, Polly moved slowly away from the window. To the hiding place.

It was such a small pile of powder to carry such finality. A teaspoon, maybe. It was strange to think that it would put an end to both Denny and herself.

Don't think about it – it's too late to think about it. She drew a deep breath. *Concentrate on the mechanics, now. One step at a time.* That was the way to go. To go –

First – she stood and gathered up the separated capsules – *dispose of the evidence.* If Sheila should find them both asleep, she'd think nothing of it. But if she found those tiny empty tell-tale cases in the rubbish, she'd know something was wrong.

They were a full handful. She fumbled to collect all the elusive bits of gelatine casings, but her hands were trembling. Some dropped, rolling over the dressing-table and on to the floor.

She stooped and gathered them up – surely that was all of them. From force of habit, she straightened slowly, although the familiar pain was missing, had been missing for some hours now. She wasn't fooled. It was just the same thing as the way a bothersome tooth stopped aching when a visit to the dentist was imminent. It was just a trick of the mind and body – not a spontaneous remission, not a cure.

She flushed the toilet, but only a portion of the capsules disappeared. At least half of them had filled with air and were bobbing mockingly in the bowl. She waited for the cistern to fill and tried once more. Again, some stubbornly refused to flush away.

Did it matter? They were only gelatine, after all, meant to dissolve in liquid. Wouldn't they just be shapeless blobs by the time Sheila got back? She'd never be able to tell what they had been – if she noticed them at all.

She pulled the chain frantically again, aware that she was half-sobbing.

'Mum? Mum?' That was Denny, drawn away from his television, coming up the stairs. 'Mum?' Worried about her. Upset, without knowing why, by the unaccustomed overactivity of the plumbing.

'It's all right, Denny.' She went to the top of the stairs. 'I'm here. I'm coming down now and make us some nice cocoa. Then we'll get to bed and have an early night.'

For a moment, Denny looked as though he might protest. He always hated going to bed early – just like a child. And nothing to be wondered about, he *was* a child. *Her* child. And she'd take care of him.

Unexpectedly, Denny capitulated without argument. 'All right,' he said docilely.

'You're a good boy, Denny,' Polly said. 'Come up and get into your pyjamas now and I'll bring up our cocoa in a minute.'

She heard him climbing the stairs as she went back into her room. *Such a good boy, such a wasted life. What couldn't he have been, if only he'd had the brain to match that fine body?*

Careful, mustn't spill any, or you might not have enough.

She picked up the saucer of powder and went downstairs into the kitchen.

Carefully, even more carefully, she carried the tray with the two cups of cocoa upstairs. And a packet of biscuits for Denny – he loved chocolate biscuits so. He could eat his fill of them tonight without reproach. So long as he drank his cocoa with them.

Denny was already in bed, the covers pulled up around him. He usually delayed, stalled, wasted time. But tonight, he'd got straight into bed, meek as a lamb.

For a moment, the old reactions swept over her and she began to worry that he was sickening for something. Perhaps she ought to check his temperature.

Then the rattle of cups from the tray in her hands brought her back to the present, to the here and now. It didn't matter if Denny *was* coming down with some illness. They neither of them were going to be here long enough for it to matter to them.

'Chocolate biscuits, Denny.' She set the tray down carefully on the bedside table. 'Your favourites. You can eat all you want tonight. It's a special treat.'

'Not hungry.' But, automatically, his hand reached out and closed around three biscuits.

'You can't drink lying down like that. Sit up now, or you'll get biscuit crumbs all in the bed.'

'I'm up! I'm up!' He wriggled to a sitting position as she bent over him, clutching the bedclothes defensively around his middle.

'Then have your cocoa.' She handed it to him, watching him take the first big gulps.

'That's right, Denny. Drink it down. It will – ' her voice shook – 'it will help you to sleep.'

Denny lowered the cup thoughtfully and took an enormous bite of one of his biscuits. She put the packet on the table beside him. 'Have all you want, Denny.' And she picked up the tray with her own cup of cocoa. If she stayed here and watched him, she'd never be able to go through with it. She'd dash the cup from his hand. And what would be the good of that? It would only mean she had the whole thing to do over again later.

In the doorway, she paused and looked back. 'Have you said your prayers tonight, Denny?'

His startled look, his quick guilty nod, told her that he hadn't. But he'd say them, now he'd been reminded.

'Don't forget to make a good Act of Contrition,' she said, and closed the door behind her.

Perhaps she ought to make one herself – in case it would do any good, in case it might mitigate any of the circumstances. But she'd come to this decision – this deliberate sin – after too much thinking and planning. Could there be any forgiveness for her under those circumstances?

'*Oh, my God, I am heartily sorry* –' As she sipped the cocoa, her mind slid into the old familiar formula – '*for having offended Thee. Because I dread the loss of heaven and the pains of hell; but, most of all* –*'* Oh, Denny, Denny.

The cup was empty, she should wash it out. But she should write a note to Sheila, too. She fumbled in the dressing-table drawer for notebook and pen.

'Dear Sheila –

'I'm sorry for having to do this to you. Try not to blame me too much –'

The letters blurred before her eyes. That stuff had never worked so fast before. Of course, she'd never taken so much of it before.

Dear God, I'm not ready! I've got to try to explain, so that Sheila can understand. I've got to –

The dressing-table tilted away from her as she fell back on the bed. The tiny part of her mind that was still conscious noted with clinical precision the onset of the heavy, stertorous breathing that meant she was sliding into a coma.

DENNY

She had gone. Denny absently took another gulp of cocoa as he listened. He heard the door of her room close and knew that she would not be stirring again tonight.

He set down his cup carefully, slightly surprised to find himself still holding the chocolate biscuits. He took another bite, cramming them all into his mouth – they were pretty crumpled up, it would just upset everybody if he tried to put them back into the packet. Mum and Sheila got awfully upset about little things like that.

Throwing back the bedclothes, he slid quietly to the floor, peeling off his pyjama jacket. It had been a tight fit over his clothes – good job Mum hadn't noticed. He'd been worried for a while, but she'd seemed to be thinking about something else.

('*Make a good Act of Contrition.*') Denny's forehead wrinkled. Did Mum know what he had been doing today? Or did she suspect that he was going to sneak out of the house tonight and go back to Merelda's?

Mum wouldn't approve, he knew. Not of any of it. Not of going to tea with Merelda, even. ('*Don't go bothering people, Denny. They've got more to do than to be bothered with the likes of you.*') But Merelda wanted him. She needed him. He was going to scare the bad man for her. With the gun. Mum wouldn't approve of that, either.

He folded the pyjama jacket neatly and placed it underneath the pillow with the pyjama trousers. He didn't bother pulling the bedclothes back into place – he'd be going straight to bed, probably, when he got back, and nobody would know.

He yawned. He was pretty tired. It had been a busy day.

Maybe some cocoa would help wake him up a little. ('*Drink it down. It will help you to sleep.*')

Denny paused in mid-swallow and let the rest of the mouthful squish between his teeth back into the cup. He couldn't go to sleep now. He had too much to do tonight.

But Mum had said to drink up his cocoa. She'd be mad when she came to call him in the morning and found he'd let it go to waste. (*It's a sin to waste good food, Denny. Lots of boys and girls all over the world would be glad to have it.*')

Of course, he'd drunk an awful lot of it. He squinted at the level of the liquid judiciously. Yes, lots. Would she really be mad if every last little bit wasn't gone?

You couldn't tell. She got upset awfully easily these days. The least little thing set her off. Maybe she'd even cry again.

He couldn't stand that. He forced another swallow down.

But he couldn't go to sleep, either. Not now. He yawned again. There was just one thing to do.

He opened the window wider. Slowly and carefully, so that it didn't make any noise. He hadn't done this since he was a real little kid.

He leaned out, holding the cup as far away from the house as possible, and tossed the remains of the cocoa into the yard below. He listened anxiously and relaxed when he heard it splash on the ground. It would have been awful if a sudden gust of wind had blown the dark liquid back against the side of the house to stain it, giving him away.

Drawing back into the room, he probed thoughtfully with his forefinger at the sludge at the bottom of the cup. Did he have time?

There was a store of sugar in one of his drawers. If you stirred a couple of spoonfuls into the residue of the cocoa, you got a delicious chocolate syrup.

Still considering this, he licked the finger. It tasted funny. Bitter. Too bitter. It would probably take all the sugar he had left to get it sweet enough. Maybe he'd better not bother.

Besides, there wasn't much time. He yawned again and reached for his airline bag. He ought to be starting on his way. If only, he rubbed his eyes, if only he just didn't feel so tired.

Maybe if he took the packet of biscuits with him, munching them might help him to stay awake. He bent over to unzip his airline bag and was suddenly, unsettlingly, dizzy.

Maybe he ought not to go out tonight, after all. Maybe he ought to go back to bed. Maybe Merelda wouldn't mind if he went and scared the bad man tomorrow night, instead.

Considering this, he lifted the airline bag on to the bed where he sat and opened it there. That was better. When he didn't have to bend over, he didn't feel so dizzy.

Although – He yawned again and reached to put the packet of biscuits into the bag. Suddenly, he was wide awake.

How had that got in there?

The soft blue chiffon clung to his fingers, the faint scent of remembered fragrance floated upwards to him. It was almost as though she were in the room with him, her tiny hands clinging to his, her greeny-blue eyes upturned trustingly.

Merelda.

Her scarf. How had it got into his bag? Had it fallen in, somehow, when she was helping him with his coat?

He pulled it completely out of the bag. A stub of tawny-gold chalk fell to the floor beside the bed. The chalk the colour of her hair. Funny though he felt, he couldn't leave it lying there. It would be like leaving Merelda lying on the floor, in a way.

Carefully, he bent and retrieved the chalk. Straightening up, dizzy and sleepy, he leaned against the bedside table. Its smooth brown surface seemed to beckon him. He wanted to rest his head on his arms and sleep.

But Merelda was waiting for him. Trusting in him. Absently, he traced the outline of her hair on the table-top, the soft curling tendrils as they had swept from her forehead to the nape of her neck, shimmering against the blue of her scarf.

Her scarf! *Was* she waiting for him so trustingly? Or had she missed her scarf? Did she, perhaps, think that he had taken it deliberately? Stolen it?

He must go to her and explain. He snatched up the airline bag, desperately ramming the scarf and biscuits into it. The stub of chalk fell back on to the floor, splintering, while the main bit rolled under the bed – he didn't notice it. He had to go to Merelda.

Opening the bedroom door, he paused and listened. No sound came from downstairs – Sheila hadn't come back yet. Across the hall, a faint rumbling – Mum was snoring. She always claimed she didn't, but now he knew better. It was too bad he couldn't wake her up and prove it, but people stopped snoring as soon as they awoke, and she wouldn't believe him.

Besides, she'd want to know why he was still up, and what he thought he was doing.

On tiptoe, he started down the stairs, but they seemed to sway under him. He caught the banister rail in time to keep from falling. More cautiously, he descended the remaining stairs.

The front door seemed an awfully long distance away. Aiming himself at it, he was aware he lurched the way the men leaving pubs lurched on Saturday nights. Did they feel as tired as he did? As sleepy and dizzy?

The door knob slid round in his hand, then caught and held, swinging the door open. He wanted so much to sleep.

Loath to leave the light and warm safety of home, he hesitated in the doorway a moment, groped for a biscuit and crammed it into his mouth, heedless that a good half of it had fallen to the floor. That helped a bit.

Merelda was waiting. He took a long, uncertain breath, and staggered towards the gate.

MERELDA

For once, she didn't waste time in the bedroom, postponing her return as long as possible. Not when he might decide to start telephoning his friends with the good news.

'I'll slip into something comfortable,' she had said, 'while you fix yourself a drink. I'll be right back.'

He was surprised when she was. Still holding the decanter, he turned to her. 'Would you like a drink – ?' He stopped abruptly, with a foolish beam. 'Or would it be bad for – ?'

'Not this early,' she said quickly. He seemed dubious and faintly disappointed. 'But perhaps,' she recovered smoothly, 'we ought to start as we mean to go on. If you could have Ethel bring me a glass of milk – ?' She might as well humour him. This performance, after all, was strictly a one-night stand.

'I'll get it myself,' he said eagerly.

The calm, practised smile didn't fade from her face, even when he left the room. She walked over to the window, looking out and down, still smiling blithely.

It was too early, of course. In the blackness of the night, the liquid black of the river glittered in the light from the street lamps.

When would he come? *Would he come at all?* She pushed that thought out of her mind. She had planned too carefully, waited too long, to fail now. He *had* to come. Tonight.

She looked down the empty street, *willing* him to come, as though the sheer force of her concentration would summon him to her.

But it was undoubtedly too early, despite the darkness. She had no idea where he lived, what his home circumstances were, how easy it would be for him to leave his home, who watched over him, and how well they watched. All unknowns, all imponderables.

She must be mad! She felt the sudden overwhelming panic again. What was she doing, placing her trust in a – a daftie? Letting the burden of her plan fall on shoulders unfit to carry it?

Perhaps she should call it off. Change her mind. Send Denny away, if he showed up. Try a reasoned, reasonable approach to Keith about a divorce –

'Here you are, then.' He stood proudly in the doorway,

bearing a tall glass of milk on a silver tray. 'Good – and good for you, as they say. Eh, lass?' He moved towards her.

No. She abandoned the brief, abortive plan. He would never let her go. Especially now, when he believed she was bearing his child.

There could never be a divorce. She had slammed that door herself when she had let him believe the lie.

There was nothing to do but go ahead with her original plan. Had she ever intended anything else? A divorce wouldn't give her enough money. This fluttering panic was simply a form of stage-fright – she had some tricky scenes ahead of her. It was a case of first-night nerves, that was all.

'Thank you, darling.' She took the glass of milk and raised it to him before drinking. His face glowed with delight.

'That's the spirit, lass.' He reached for his own drink and joined her. 'To us.' His arm circled her waist, his hand patted her stomach gently. '*All* of us.'

She kept smiling.

'*Anyone who marries for money earns it,*' her mother had always said smugly, secure in the delusion that she was happy in her slum because 'love' was – or had been – there. Despising her for the platitude and the delusion, the constant cheap sentimentality, Merelda made her own choice . . . earned her money. It was the continuing to earn it, through the long years stretching out ahead, she shrank from . . . would not face.

'Aah, lass –' he looked out at the glittering river view – 'we've come a far piece from our beginnings, both of us. We've got a wonderful life to offer our children. They'll never have to go through the struggles we've had. It's all here, waiting for them.'

She moved away, smoothly and unhurriedly. Back in command of herself. *Act III, Scene I.* The panic was over, just as suddenly, she was sure that Denny would come.

'I think I ought to rest a bit.' She sank gracefully into

an armchair, curling her feet up.

'Good idea, good idea. Shall I get you a blanket? Anything you'd like?'

Only the entrance of Denny . . . with the gun. Smiling, she shook her head.

'The television? The hi-fi? Yes, we'll put some records on.' He looked up from the record rack, radiant with a new thought. 'We'll have to get some more records — nursery rhymes, stories and such-like. For the baby.'

'There's plenty of time yet.' She smiled, indulging him. His time was nearly gone.

Denny was on the way.

SHEILA

She was later than she had intended to be. First, she had gone past the doctor's surgery, but it was dark and closed. That meant she'd have to try in the morning, after all.

Then the library — and the last person in the world she felt like encountering again today. Aunt Vera. Voluble and vociferous, and not to be denied. Not to be shaken off, either.

Vera was beside her now, insistent on coming back home with her to see how Mum was feeling after her visit to the doctor. It was no use telling her Mum had gone to bed early and wouldn't like to be disturbed.

'I won't disturb her. I'll just peek in, and if she's not awake, I'll come right out again.'

Translated, Sheila knew, that meant Vera would hover in the doorway, shuffling her feet and clearing her throat until Mum woke. Once her rest had been disturbed, Mum often didn't get back to sleep again that night. You'd think Aunt Vera would realize that, being a nurse. But Sheila had often noticed that people in medicine had one code for their patients and quite another for their families.

'Honestly, Aunt Vera —' she had to try — 'it would be

better to let Mum sleep tonight – '

'Didn't I just say I would?' There were times – becoming more frequent recently – when every conversational road with Vera led to an argument.

'If she's taken her pill, I suppose she won't wake up, anyway.' It was surrender – and Vera knew it. She pounced triumphantly.

'Of course she won't. And *I'll* sleep better for satisfying myself that she's all right. She gave us all a nasty turn today. Collapsing like that. She ought to – '

Disconnecting her attention (she'd heard it all before – or else something so nearly like it that she could make responses in the right places without even noticing that she was doing so), Sheila turned the corner abruptly. As though, by veering sharply enough, she could cause Vera to break away and go spinning out of her orbit.

Hopeless, of course. Her footsteps quickened, but that was hopeless, too. Vera kept pace effortlessly. Sheila forced herself to slow down, she was almost running. That was silly. As silly as this ridiculous feeling sweeping over her that something was wrong somewhere.

They turned a final corner. Sheila made one last desperate attempt to throw off Vera. 'Would you like to stop and – '

'The door's open!' Vera said. 'You went out and left the front door open!'

'No!' Sheila denied she had left the front door open, tried to deny that it was open at all. But the sharp sliver of light cut into the night like a sword blade. The door *was* open. Something *was* wrong.

They were both running now, not wasting any more words. In a last-minute spurt, Sheila outdistanced Vera and gained the hallway ahead of her. A biscuit crunched underneath her feet as she entered.

'How you could have been so careless – ' Vera would always have enough breath left to scold. 'Thieves could have come in and carried away the whole house – ' She looked around, obviously dissatisfied that the house was still there, that nothing was even missing from the hallway.

Still dissatisfied, she peered hopefully into the parlour.

If I didn't leave the front door open – and I didn't – the thought formed reluctantly in Sheila's mind – *then who did?*

There could be only one answer. *Denny.*

Vera whirled suspiciously, plucking the thought out of the air. 'Where's Denny?' she demanded.

'In his room.' Sheila hoped it was the truth. 'I suppose,' she added weakly.

'We'll see about that.' Vera started up the stairs. Sheila had to follow, praying that Denny would be there.

He wasn't, of course. How else could the door have been open?

'I knew it!' Vera said. 'It's come to *this*!' Her tone put Denny out lurking in some bushes, intent upon ravishment and rape.

'Nothing of the sort!' Sheila flared to his defence, but keeping her voice low, mindful of Mum's closed door. Mum needed all the rest she could get. With luck, this might be sorted out without disturbing her.

'Where *is* he, then? I always warned Polly this would happen some day. Letting him have his head as much as she did, letting him roam anywhere in the city –' She started for the closed bedroom door with the light of righteous battle in her eyes.

'Aunt Vera.' Sheila stepped in front of her. 'Please, Aunt Vera, let Mum sleep. Denny won't have gone far – not at this hour. He's afraid of the dark. We can find him ourselves.'

She watched. Vera hesitated, torn between the desire for an immediate confrontation with her sister-in-law and the thought of the additional satisfaction she would find in bursting into the bedroom with the errant Denny in tow. Aunt Vera didn't realize it yet, but she wasn't going to get into Mum's bedroom tonight, except over Sheila's dead body.

'He can't have gone far,' Sheila said again, enticingly. 'Look, there's his empty cup of cocoa. And he'd been in bed. It's been slept in. Perhaps he just thought he heard a bird chirping that had fallen out of its nest, or a puppy crying, and went out to look.' There had been a time when they'd had trouble with him over things like that. It might be starting up again.

'That's nonsense,' Vera sniffed. 'Polly ought to know immediately –'

'But it wouldn't be nonsense to Denny. It's just the sort of thing he worries about when he wakes up at night. Come on.' Sheila moved towards the stairs. 'We'll go out and check the yard, and up and down the street.'

Vera began to move, then stopped, her snapping eyes fixed on the bedside table. 'He's getting destructive, too,' she said portentously. 'Look at that table. He's scrawled all over it. I tell you, he's taken some kind of fit, and Polly –'

'You know she ought to sleep.'

'Ah, but *is* she sleeping? She might be lying awake in there. In which case, it won't do her any harm to get up and help us find him.'

The first part of it was true. Mum *might* be lying awake in there, shrinking from the sound of Vera's voice. Hiding, trusting to Sheila to get rid of Vera for the night.

'Look,' Sheila said desperately, 'I'll just peek inside the door and see if she *is* asleep. If she isn't, all right. But, if she is, then we'll let her rest and try to find Denny ourselves first. All right?'

'All right,' Vera said grudgingly, still brooding over the chalked-up bedside table. 'And *that* will get ground into the carpet.' She swooped on fragments of tawny-gold chalk, sweeping them into her hand and depositing them on the table. 'I know you and Polly don't like to think that you can't manage him by yourselves, but the time is coming when you're going to have to face facts and be sensible.' She began rubbing at the chalk scrawls. 'There's no excuse for this sort of behaviour, it's some sort of regression. Once, you had all this destructiveness trained out of him.'

Heart sinking (might it be true? Denny used to be so good about property), Sheila opened Mum's door noiselessly and stood just outside, listening.

She'd been prepared to lie, to protect Polly from Aunt Vera (she'd had enough of her for one day), but it wasn't necessary. Mum's deep, heavy breathing was proof that she was honestly in a sound slumber, the slumber she needed so badly. That was good. Vera should *not* disturb her tonight.

'She's sound asleep.' Sheila closed the door firmly behind her, prepared to protect Mum's precious slumber by force, if necessary. God send that it might not be necessary – Aunt Vera would never forgive rough hands laid upon her. Nor let anyone forget them, either. 'Let's go downstairs and see if Denny's outside. He'll be somewhere nearby.' She spoke with a confidence she did not entirely feel.

'He'd better be.' Vera reluctantly descended the stairs with her. The front door was still invitingly ajar; but Denny, if he was out there, hadn't accepted the invitation. They were going to have to hunt for him. And he might be anywhere – a fact she was not prepared to admit to Vera.

'You go that way,' Sheila said, as they paused outside the gate, 'and I'll cross the street and circle the block the other way. He'll be around here somewhere.'

Vera sniffed disbelievingly. 'If *I* find him, I'll give him a piece of my mind. Running off like this, causing us all this worry and grief. He used to know better, but he's . . .' Her voice faded away as she moved off.

Sheila crossed the street, straining her eyes against the darkness. *Denny, Denny, where are you? Don't let it be true – any of what Aunt Vera's thinking. Oh, God! – please don't let it be true!*

She turned the corner, the street was empty. So deserted there might never have been anyone on it. Even the houses seemed empty and withdrawn, few showing any lights, and those few illumined only by the eerie blue glow of a television screen.

She was shivering now, not just with the cold. Suppose they didn't find him, where could they begin to look?

Of course – she tried for calm common sense – he'd come home on his own – eventually. There was no real reason for this terrifying sense of urgency. It was just that

Vera was kicking up such a fuss. Right now, Vera was planning to burst in on Mum, startle her out of the first good night's sleep she'd had in weeks, and create a scene. And that – Sheila's mouth tightened – just couldn't be allowed to happen.

She had turned another corner and, ahead of her, saw the dark outline of a man. A big man, tall enough to be Denny, and with something familiar about him.

She started to run. On tiptoe, so as not to frighten him. Poor Denny, in the darkness every unexpected sound was a new menace to him. It was a wonder that he had brought himself to go out at all.

Keeping her eyes on him, she slowed, then stopped. Something was wrong. She'd let hope deceive her. She stood there and watched him crossing the street.

He walked slowly, but confidently, his arms swinging slightly at his side, his steps controlled and precise. A man who walked like that was a man who knew where he was going and why. A man who walked like that was all of a piece.

It wasn't Denny's walk.

She turned the final corner. That street was empty, too. As she neared her own street, she could see Vera approaching it from the opposite direction. Vera saw her, too, but didn't pause to wait for her, just kept hurrying along. Was Vera going to try to get to Mum before she could reach the house herself?

Sheila broke into a run again, not caring how much noise she made this time, but Vera was standing in the doorway.

'No sign of him,' she said. 'I told you so!'

'He wouldn't have gone far,' Sheila said stubbornly. 'Perhaps he's come back while we've been gone.'

'I don't believe *that*,' Vera said, 'and neither do you. It's time to wake Polly and let her know what's going on. If we don't, and something happens, she'll never forgive us.'

Because that was true, too, Sheila looked up the stairs, aching to see Denny smiling sleepily like a naughty child at the top. Longing for it all to turn out to be just a tempest in a teapot – which it could never be with Aunt Vera intent on mixing it.

'Can't we at least look?' Sheila insisted. Disregarding Vera's shrug of scepticism, she walked over to glance into the parlour and then, snapping on the light, the kitchen, before returning to join Vera in the hallway. Vera hadn't moved.

'He might be upstairs,' Sheila said, 'back in his own room. He wouldn't know we'd been looking for him.'

Too eagerly, Vera started up the stairs. Sheila was right behind her, ready to cut her off if she turned in the wrong direction. At the top of the stairs, Sheila moved up, blocking her off from Mum's room. Reluctantly, Vera turned into Denny's room. It was still empty.

'You see?' Vera crowed. 'There's nothing for it, but to let Polly know – '

'We haven't looked in my room,' Sheila said frantically. 'Or on the roof. He might have gone up on the roof.'

'It was the *front* door that was open,' Vera reminded her.

'He might have gone outside and seen something on the roof, or thought he did. We ought to look.' Almost convincing herself, Sheila herded Vera ahead of her, up the second flight of stairs.

He wasn't in Sheila's room and Vera balked at going farther. 'You know perfectly well there's nobody up on that roof. I'm not going up there.'

What Sheila knew perfectly well was that, if she left Vera alone, Vera would sneak down into Mum's room as soon as her back was turned.

'We can't be sure,' she said. 'Come with me just as far as the roof door,' she added craftily. 'You can wait there while I go out on the roof. I – I'd like you there – just in case . . .'

'Oh, well.' Vera rose to the bait Sheila felt like a traitor to Denny for offering. 'In for a penny, in for a pound, I suppose.'

The swathe of light from the open door slashed across the roof and Sheila could see no one was there. Nevertheless, she went out, moving cautiously to the edge to look down into the deserted street. No sign of Denny anywhere.

'*I told you so*' was in the air when she went back to the doorway, but Vera didn't voice it this time. She had her triumph and that was enough to be getting on with. The next battle was to be with Polly – and that was the one that must be averted.

As slowly as she dared, Sheila descended the stairs, while Vera fumed behind her. She paused irresolutely at the landing, wondering how to keep Vera away from Polly. 'Let's go down to the kitchen and have a cup of tea,' she offered, without any real hope.

'This is no time for tea,' Vera snapped.

Half agreeing with her, Sheila hesitated. Down below, the door bell pealed.

'It's Denny!' Sheila flew down the remaining flight of stairs. 'He's come home!' She flung open the front door. 'Where have you been? Everybody's been worried sick – '

'Is anything wrong here?' A tall, pleasant-faced young man stood there. 'I saw all the lights, and someone out on the roof. I wondered if there was anything I could do. It's all right,' he added, 'I'm a friend of Denny's and – '

Upstairs, Vera screamed sharply. Just once.

DENNY

It certainly was dark. And cold. No moon. No stars. And it was probably going to rain any minute. Denny pulled his coat tighter, but it didn't seem to do much good. Some of the cold was right there inside of him, where the coat couldn't make any difference.

But there was still an awfully long way to go. It never seemed so far in the daylight. Maybe it wouldn't be so bad if he wasn't so awfully sleepy. He couldn't stop yawning.

Away back, somewhere in the streets behind him, he'd passed an old tramp, dozing comfortably in a doorway.

There had been an almost overwhelming temptation to
join him – or to find a sheltered doorway of his own. Denny
had had to fight it hard. It would have upset Mum more
than anything. (Once they'd passed someone like that,
when they were out walking. '*Look at that, Denny. Dis-
graceful, that's what it is. How anyone could forget themselves so far –* ' Her voice had choked off strangely, and
she had added, even more strangely, '*You'll never end up
like that, Denny. Never. I promise you.*')

No, he couldn't find a nice doorway of his own. Mum
would never forgive him.

He had to stay awake and keep going on, instead. Not
only because of Mum, but because of Merelda, who
needed him. But he was so awfully tired. He couldn't
remember ever being so sleepy before. His footsteps slowed,
he leaned against a telephone kiosk. Maybe, if he rested
a minute, he would feel better.

There wasn't much in the airline bag, but it weighed his
arm down so heavily it might have been filled with stones.
Slowly, he drew it up and rummaged in it. If he ate a few
more biscuits, they might help to keep him awake. And it
would make the bag lighter, too.

Mouth full, he closed his eyes for a moment against
the dizziness. He was dizzy now, even when standing upright, not just when he bent over. ('*Time to go to bed,
Denny. Look at you – you're dead on your feet.*') But there
was no bed to go to – bed was a long, long way off –
there was only the cold hard concrete of the pavement at
his feet. He felt himself imperceptibly sliding towards it
and opened his eyes with an effort.

More biscuit. He crammed it into his mouth. It wasn't
working as well as he thought it would. Maybe he was too
tired. But it wasn't terribly late. Maybe he was coming
down with 'flu, or something. Mum would know. Mum
could take his temperature and tell him just what was
the matter with him. Mum would take care of him – give
him something to make him better. Mum would always
take care of him. But Mum was a long way away, too.

The faster he got to Merelda and carried out his promise

to her, the sooner he could get home to Mum. He pushed himself away from the kiosk, and tried to tidy his airline bag in the dim light from the old-fashioned street lamp. His fingers curled around some loose pieces of chalk at the bottom of the bag and he pulled them out to look at them. There weren't many left. Tomorrow he must try to find Rembrandt again and see if he could get some more. Rembrandt had lots of chalks that were wearing low – too low to use properly.

One of the chalk pieces stayed in his hand as he re-zipped the bag. His fingers curled around it, finding reassurance in the smooth powdery feel of it. He squinted down at it, but it seemed to blur and dissolve before his eyes, although he could still feel it in his hand. His hand was blurred, too.

He blinked hard, two or three times, and the world cleared and came into focus again. He was all right. To prove it, he tried a few experimental strokes with the chalk against the building. The colour was right – it was the last of his tawny-gold chalks – the lines curved recognizably into the curl and sweep of Merelda's hair. Absently, he sketched in the outline of her profile.

Merelda. He had to get to her. Help her. And then, maybe – the street ahead of him dipped and swirled – she could help him. He'd never felt quite so awful before. His vision began to blur again.

He moved slowly, pushing himself away from the building and carefully circling round the telephone kiosk, watching as his feet automatically took up the tempo of his long, loping stride. They were doing it by themselves, because he wasn't concentrating enough to direct them. He was only watching them, in case they blurred and dissolved, like the rest of the world, and let him slide down sprawling on to the pavement. Everything felt so strange, looked so strange – he was beginning to be afraid.

Voices carried to him on the clear night air. Two girls were coming towards him. As he looked up, he could see them clearly, recognize them. They were old friends. Once, maybe a long time ago now, they had all played together. Then they'd gone off to school, the way most of the other children did, and he hadn't seen them again. Not until now.

Beaming, he raised his hand in greeting, and hurried towards them. 'Hello. How are – ?'

They crossed the street. Looking back nervously over their shoulders, they walked faster and faster, until they were almost running.

He had started after them, but now he stopped. Maybe they didn't remember him. Maybe it was all longer ago than he'd thought – that happened sometimes. He seemed to remember people better than they remembered him. Especially girls. It was something to do with the way time got all muddled. (*'Don't bother your head about it, Denny.'*)

They had reached the far corner now, and looked back at him one last time. Hopefully, he waved to them. But that made them really run – he could hear their pounding footsteps long after they were out of sight.

He turned slowly – the world was wavering around him again – to continue his journey. Steadying himself against a wall, he got as far as the turning before the dizziness forced him to stop and rest for a moment.

He wished he'd never started out now, he wasn't getting any better. But he'd gone too far to turn back. He was closer to Merelda's than to home. He had to go on. Then Merelda would help him.

He pushed himself away from the wall, sighted carefully at the spot across the road he must reach, and started forward.

From a great distance, he heard a squealing of brakes, and a furious voice shouting, 'Why don't you watch where you're going?' It was all a long way off and could have nothing to do with him.

He gained the opposite pavement and headed for the river, intent upon his purpose. Merelda was waiting.

SHEILA

Upstairs, Vera screamed just once. Forgetting the stranger at the door, Sheila whirled and dashed upstairs, only vaguely aware that he was right behind her.

She stopped in the doorway and he pushed past her into the room. 'Aunt Vera!' she gasped. Polly was lying, fully dressed, on the bed. Vera was pulling at her and slapping her face with light brisk slaps.

'Ambulance!' Vera snapped, not looking up. Sheila stood there frozen, staring.

'Telephone?' the man asked.

'Downstairs!' He bolted for the door, pushing Sheila aside.

'Aunt Vera, what is it?'

'I knew something was wrong,' Vera said grimly. 'But I didn't think she'd be fool enough to try this. Go and make some black coffee – strong.'

They were the last words Vera addressed to her directly. Sheila hesitated a moment, not wanting to realize what was happening – what had happened – then turned and fled for the kitchen.

Waiting for the coffee to perk, Sheila hovered between the kitchen and the bottom of the stairs. The man had ordered the ambulance and returned to Vera. She could hear Vera giving him directions.

Strange, how reluctant she had been to have Vera come back to the house with her, and now there was no one she would rather have had here. Aunt Vera had come into her own in a crisis. Vera, in her element; Vera, doing her thing – for her own family, this time.

The ambulance arrived just as the percolator began to gurgle. Sheila led the stretcher-bearers upstairs. Aunt Vera stood aside as they lifted Mum on to the stretcher. Mum, looking so marble-cold already, only the rasping agonized breaths to show that she was still there, that they mustn't stop hoping yet.

'I'll go with them,' Vera said to the stranger standing by the dressing-table. He was looking down at the carpet, then he stooped and picked something up. He straightened with it, holding it out to Vera.

'Do you know what she's taken?' he asked.

'I do that,' Vera said grimly. 'I've seen her prescription for those many a time.' Her gaze moved to the cup on the dressing-table. 'She'll have taken them in the cocoa, I suppose.'

The man sniffed at the cup, dipped a finger into the dregs at the bottom, and tasted it with the tip of his tongue. 'That's it,' he said. 'Loaded with the stuff. Any idea how much she could have taken?'

'She got the prescription re-filled tonight.' Sheila fought for control of her shaking voice. 'She had a full bottle.'

'And Lord knows how many capsules saved from other bottles,' Vera said. 'I knew she wasn't taking them properly. She wasn't fooling me.'

'She's going to be all right, isn't she?' Mum had to be. Anything else was unthinkable. Sheila watched Vera anxiously, something deep within her mind warring with a surfacing realization that was even more unthinkable. Unconsciously, she fought against the knowledge.

'We'll do everything we can.' Vera turned to follow the stretcher out of the room. 'There's no guarantee.'

But something else was without a guarantee. Something to do with the pills and the cocoa. Why had Mum bothered to take all those capsules apart, when she'd known she was going to take them? Wouldn't it have been easier to have swallowed them whole? Why go to all that bother?

'Have you seen this note?' The man was holding it out to her. 'It's addressed to you.'

She took it, glancing at the few straggling lines which suddenly conveyed to her what the words themselves did not.

'Oh, God – Denny!' She dashed across the hall, into the empty room and stood staring down at the cocoa dregs in the bottom of his empty cup. Half-way down the stairs,

Vera halted and came back.

It wasn't necessary for the man to test those dregs, tasting lightly with the tip of his tongue, as he had done in Mum's room. She *knew*. Before he even nodded agreement, she *knew*.

It was why the capsules had been emptied, the powder carefully mixed into the cocoa. So that poor, innocent Denny would drink unsuspectingly. *She was going to take him with her.*

'Where *is* he?' the man asked urgently. 'Where's Denny?'

'Oh, God! – I don't know!' Fighting for control, she saw the expression on Vera's face – and, in a curious way, that helped. It crystallized the anguished despair into a cold fury, through which she could think.

'He's gone out. Somewhere. I don't know where.' That was why the house was alight, with the brightness and movement which had drawn this helpful stranger to their door. 'We came home and found him gone. We've been out looking for him, but we didn't find him.' Because they had been looking for him in the wrong places? Looking to see him walking along the pavement, when he might already have slumped down into some shadows to sleep – and die?

'Oh, God – !' The hysteria was slipping out of control again. 'We've *got* to find him. He can't be just left to die out there.' She rushed wildly to the window, opening it and leaning out. The whole bleak, enormous world was outside – and he could be anywhere in it. 'We've got to find him. We need help. Call the police!'

'It's all right.' The man patted her shoulder as he turned away to go downstairs to the telephone again. 'I *am* the police.'

Other police had come and gone, greeting Peter jocularly as they entered, asking him if he couldn't keep away from work – even when he was off duty and in plain clothes. She had watched their grins and his embarrassment as he had tried to explain, in an off-hand way, that he'd met Mrs O'Magnon coming along the road earlier in the evening and something about her manner had – well, he'd been uneasy and thought it would do no harm to walk past the house and check that everything was all right. (Funny, the way men hated to admit to intuition, even when they called it a hunch.) Only then the other policemen had glanced at her and stopped grinning. There was nothing funny about it now.

Peter was still here with her, firmly identified now as Denny's friend, 'Constable Pete', often spoken of, never met. He was helpful and friendly, trying to shield her from the others. It was impossible in a house that size, of course. She'd overheard most of what they'd been saying.

Some of the others hadn't been so nice. Pleasant enough, but remote. Of necessity, armoured in their uniforms against the people they had to meet and deal with in their job. They'd taken away the cups and Mum's note. They'd started the search for Denny. They'd tried to be kind, to keep their voices low, but some words just leaped into your ears.

Words like 'murder', 'diminished responsibility', 'manslaughter'. It was hard to realize that they were talking about Mum and Denny. That they were taking it so calmly, that they'd seen it all before.

This, then, was what Officialdom meant when it released long reports about most murders being committed within families. It meant the endless strain of one person looking after another, without hope of relief or recovery, through age and illness, until they couldn't go on any more. Until one of them had to die – or both of them. It meant Mum and Denny.

It meant, too, the ones who stood by and let it happen. Too accustomed to the situation to notice the gradual changes, too stupid to be able to read the signs of growing desperation. Like herself. And it meant the others – not so close – who could see that something was increasingly wrong, but believed that what eventually happened would be for the best. Like Vera.

She'd seen the look in Vera's eyes. (*May God forgive you for it, Vera O'Magnon – I can't.*) The look that said,

'*Maybe it's all for the best*,' when they knew Denny had drunk that drugged cocoa before he left the house – and disappeared.

Vera would let it happen. She wouldn't push the search for Denny. She was hoping they wouldn't find him until it was too late. Because he wasn't 'right', because she felt he reflected on the precious family honour, because it would 'make things easier', she would let him die. He was out there, lost and alone, not knowing what was happening to him. But Vera would rather they didn't find him. She'd let him crawl into the bushes and die like some animal – and then she'd call it '*God's mercy*'.

'I can't just sit here!' Sheila stood up. 'I've got to go out. Look for him. He *must* be somewhere near here.'

The young policewoman got up, too, and moved forward, but Peter shook his head. 'It's all right,' he said, 'I've been thinking the same thing myself. You stay here to take messages or in case he comes back. We can go out and look.'

Sheila started towards him, then stopped. 'Look *where*?' The enormity of the task overwhelmed her, even as she knew she'd gladly walk her feet down to the ankles just to have the illusion of actively doing something. 'He could be anywhere.'

'I've had a thought about that myself,' Peter said. 'Let's just take another look upstairs.'

She followed him up the stairs and into Denny's room. It seemed emptier and more poignant every time she entered it. Tears were too close and she fought them away. They could do no good. Time enough for tears when every last hope had been exhausted. When there was nothing else to be done.

'There,' Peter said, pointing triumphantly at the bedside table. There was nothing on it except the last trace of Denny alive – the chalky squiggles Vera had tried to erase. (As she'd see Denny erased, without compunction, so that the surface of her life would be smooth and unmarred again.)

'And – ' he knelt, plunged under the bed and surfaced

with a stub of chalk, ' – there.' Standing, he matched it to the chalk marks on the table-top. They were the same colour. 'That's what I thought.'

'What is?' The chalk conveyed nothing to her except the memory of the times Denny had been scolded for using it heedlessly on the pavement just outside the house. And sometimes on the walls. It was useless now to regret the times she'd scolded him, but she couldn't help it. She was conscious of the onset of self-recrimination – as though Denny were already dead and the work of mourning him had started. Had something inside her accepted the finality of it already?

'This gives us a clue to what Denny was thinking about when he started out,' Peter said. 'He gets these chalks from the pavement artist – the one he calls Rembrandt. He saw him today. Perhaps he's gone to see him again. Rembrandt might have invited him round – '

'But Denny never goes out at night – ' She broke off the protest. It no longer applied. Denny *had* gone out tonight. Somewhere. 'Do you really think so?'

'Depend on it.' He was jubilant. 'Denny was sitting here, thinking about what he was going to do, and his hand just followed the train of his thought – and left a trail for us. That's where we'll find him. At Rembrandt's.'

'Rembrandt's.' His assurance carried her along. 'But do you know where that is?'

'It's not too far from here,' he said. 'Not too near, but not too far. Denny could have made it easily. Come on – ' he pocketed the bit of chalk – 'we'll find him there.'

MERELDA

Outside, on the river, a barge hooted with the haunting, mournful note only achieved by boats and trains en route to some lonely destination through unperceived surroundings. The banshee note of a lost soul calling out for rest and forgiveness.

Merelda shivered. He was quick to note it. 'Are you still cold? Shall we have another log on the fire?'

'No, it's all right.' She gave a light laugh. 'Just . . . someone walked over my grave.' (*Or yours.*) She laughed again.

'Don't say things like that!' But he smiled at her laughter. So long as she was happy, he was pleased. 'We'll have another log, anyway. Fire's dying down.'

(*Everything's dying tonight.*) She stilled the burble of laughter – he'd think she was hysterical. Perhaps she was. So close to the end of her goal, the triumph was hard to contain. But she must call upon the discipline she had learned so well and keep it within bounds. The hardest scenes were yet to be played. She must be ready for them.

Sparks shot up the chimney like fireworks as he tossed more wood on to the dying blaze. 'That's better.' He poked at the fire and stood up, dusting his hands. 'Shall we have the curtains drawn, then? That will make it seem warmer, too.' He started for the window.

'No, don't,' she said quickly. She wanted to be able to glance out occasionally and see if there were any sign of Denny. 'I . . . I like the view.'

'Too dark to see much.' But he turned away, leaving the curtains open.

'You can see a lot.' She crossed to the window and stood looking out. The dark glass reflected her as a wraith floating in mid-air. She leaned forward, head touching the window, and wraith and flesh united, Siamese twins, conjoined at the forehead.

Below, a Rolls glided silently along the deserted street. A thin white mist was rising from the river. Shadows stirred, advancing and retreating as a faint wind rippled the trees. Too soon? Surely, it must be time for him to come – if he were coming at all tonight.

'Aye.' A bulkier wraith swam up beside the slender one hovering in the dark glass, there were quadruplets now, joined at hips and shoulders. 'You can see more than you'd expect. Not for long, though. Getting foggy.'

Was there movement at the far end of the street? A darker shadow just beyond the street lamp? And had it been noticed? She glanced sideways quickly, but Keith's face was impassive as he stared out at the river. In any case, he could place no construction on the meaning of that shadow. Not until it came nearer.

She turned away abruptly. He followed, as she had intended. He must be kept away from the window too. He must not look out to recognize that shambling figure advancing down the street, or groping for the key beneath the flower-pot. He must not be forewarned . . . forearmed.

She chose the couch, rather than a chair, knowing that he would sit beside her. He did so immediately, no further interest in the window. She was the beacon which drew him. It was all going well, just as she had planned.

She leaned back against the cushions, smiling, and allowed herself a faint contented sigh.

'Happy, lass?'

'Oh, yes,' she said truthfully. 'I can't remember when I've been so happy.'

'Eh, lass.' He reached for her hand. 'So am I.'

She squeezed his hand abstractedly, concentrating on what was happening outside. Had Denny had time to reach the steps yet? Would he find the key? . . . The gun?

Nervously, her other hand crept up to pluck at a ruffle on her negligee. A thread gave unexpectedly and the lace began to drop away from the chiffon. She pulled her hand away, then, after a moment's reflection, let it creep back. Who would know that the lace hanging loose was the result of a pulled thread and not a struggle? It could look very sinister to a simple mentality. She began to work at separating the lace.

Was that a sound from outside? A grating of earthenware flower-pot against cement steps? She glanced at Keith again. Was it noticeable, or only audible to her because she was waiting, attuned to the sound? And if Denny were so noisy just retrieving the key, how much noise would he make opening the front door . . . pulling out the desk drawer for the gun . . . coming up the stairs?

The record ended and machinery whirred softly as the needle arm swung back to repeat. Keith stirred. 'Want to hear it again?'

'Not really,' she said. 'Play something else. That American rock musical – I'd like to hear that.'

He made a face, but went to pull the record from the rack and set it on the turntable.

She relaxed as the first grinding, blaring notes shook through the room. That would cover any lesser noise from the floor below. Workmen could tear up the street outside with hydraulic drills and it would not be noticed until the record ended. Denny could be as noisy as he liked now.

SHEILA

Leaving the house was the worst. Running the gauntlet of the curious, huddled outside the gate. Drawn by the unusual activity, the ambulance, the uniformed police coming and going at the O'Magnon house, a cordon of neighbours, reinforced by idlers and passers-by, stood watch. An emergency always enlivened the street, bringing out faces seldom seen except at Christmas and Easter Masses. The old and the infirm predominated, gleeful at having witnessed another disaster, eager to discover who it was they had outlived this time. Even the indifferent, anxious to escape involvement but still curious, lingered in half-open doors, cardigans thrown over their shoulders, ready to advance if it should seem worth their while, but equally ready to withdraw and slam the door safely behind them if there were any danger they might be asked to do something.

She tried to close her ears to the comments and Peter took her arm and hurried her through the crowd. 'What's happened?' 'Are they taking her away, too, then?' 'Is it the boy?' 'Taken a fit, has he?' 'Tried to do away with his mother, they say.' 'Did he hurt the girl, too?' 'She's walking all right.' 'Doesn't look too well.' 'Shock, probably.'

Peter's grasp tightened on her arm. Once he slowed, as though he might be going to stop and order the crowd to disperse. Then he urged her forward at a quicker pace, to get her beyond the range of the voices. Strange, the way people seemed to think they couldn't be heard as they commented on her even while she was passing them. Did they imagine they were invisible and inaudible? Or did they think that being in the centre of the drama cut her off from the rest of humanity in some way, enclosed her behind a glass wall?

They were beyond the gathering at the gate now, but, as she looked upwards at Peter's set face swiftly, he was still hurrying her along. It was kind of him, but did he really think she was hearing anything she hadn't heard before? Anything she hadn't lived with all her life?

Because it always came back to Denny. Sadly, inevitably. In a way, Aunt Vera was the voice of the community. The spokesman for all their half-formed fears and terrors of the unknown. And Denny was an unknown force to them. Poor Denny, just because he had grown so big, while his mind remained so small. Poor, innocent Denny. Except that, for them, innocence ended at a height of three-foot-six. After that, menace began to grow.

'Are you all right?' Peter asked anxiously. She nodded. They were well past the crowd now, but twitching curtains in the windows along the street still marked their progress.

'We turn here,' he said. Thankfully, they were past all the curious now, plunging into the anonymity of dark uncaring streets. 'It isn't far,' he assured her.

Dampness and swirling wisps of mist told her they were nearing the river. Instinctively, she looked around. The river had always held a fatal fascination for Denny. (*Fatal? Oh, no – not that. Not a sodden bundle of clothes bobbing along on the currents of the river, to be pulled out by some boatman, or cast up by the tide on some slimy, muddy bank.*) Denny was with Rembrandt. He had to be. Safe and warm, talking happily to one of his friends. And they'd take him to hospital – get him there in time.

'Nearly there,' he encouraged. They turned inland, but the spectre of the river still haunted her. A barge hooted mournfully, the sound eddying along with the mist and damp. She shivered, although she was not conscious of the cold. She was beyond physical discomfort.

Rembrandt lived in a basement flat in the middle of a decaying Georgian terrace. Sheila kept close to the railings as they walked down the street, peering down into the stairwells of other basement flats along the way. If Denny had been dizzy as he came this way, lost his balance, he could have fallen into one of them. Any pit of black shadows might conceal a sleeping – dying – Denny.

'Mind the steps, they're crumbling away to nothing. All these places need to be restored – or pulled down.' Peter led the way down steps into the dark area and rang the bell. Nothing happened. He tried again, then gave it up and knocked.

They could see light through a gap where the curtains didn't quite meet. At least, someone was here. Sheila hadn't realized how much she had been fearing a dead end until she felt some of the tension ease.

When the door opened abruptly, she was unprepared. She had expected an elderly man – pavement artists were a vanishing tribe – not someone young and really rather handsome. Nor had she expected someone not quite sober. There was a glass of red wine in his hand and he gestured with it as he waved them into the flat. A new worry occupied her suddenly. He hadn't been teaching Denny to drink, had he?

'Enter, friends,' he said. 'You *are* my friends, aren't you?' He squinted at them muzzily. 'Of course, you are. All the world is my friend tonight.'

The hallway was dark and cramped. They hurried past him into the big front room. It was totally a studio, canvases piled in corners and leaning against every wall. Only a couch in one corner near an open doorway, through which could be seen a tiny kitchen, was a concession to the necessary mechanics of living. The room seemd to be crowded with people staring out from canvases; jammed with scenes and landscapes of other worlds.

'Excuse the mess,' Rembrandt said pleasantly, although he now seemed faintly puzzled. 'An informal selection committee of one has been sitting, choosing pictures for an exhibition. That's right – an exhibition. The letter came this afternoon. A West End gallery has agreed to give me a one man show. It may be the beginning of – '

'Where's Denny?' Sheila interrupted. He'd go on all night if she didn't, you could see that. He was so bound up in himself that he'd no thought for anyone else right now. And she had a dreadful sinking feeling in the pit of her stomach that had begun when she looked around this room and saw no other living soul in it.

'I beg your pardon?' He blinked and seemed to see them for the first time. Intruders into his reverie. Real, not some imaginary people to applaud his story. 'Do I know you?'

'You know me,' Peter said.

'So, I do. So, I do.' Rembrandt came closer, looking at him sharply. 'It's old "Move along" himself. Well – ' he pulled a letter from among a stack of canvases and waved it triumphantly – 'I'm moving along now. Next stop, the West End – and not on any pavement, either.'

'Congratulations,' Peter said. 'You'll do well, I'm – '

'Where's Denny?' Sheila demanded urgently. Precious time was ticking away. Irretrievable time. Moments which could mean the difference between life and death for Denny.

'Denny?' Rembrandt turned to her blankly.

'Dennis O'Magnon. This is Miss O'Magnon – his sister, Sheila.' Peter made the introduction. 'We're looking for Denny. Denny – *you* know.'

Even Peter. That was the way people always identified Denny. 'Denny – *you* know.' With a significant lift of an eyebrow, or a swift gesture to temple with finger. It was another thing she had long been accustomed to, but which grated badly on her nerves tonight.

'Yes, Denny-*you*-know!' Her Irish temper flared suddenly and she made no effort to control it. 'Denny-the-dimwit. Denny-the-idiot. Denny-the-mental-defective. Or, how about, Denny-but-for-the-grace-of-God-goes-your-selves? Do you have to talk about him that way? He *is* still human, you know.'

'Yes, I know,' Rembrandt said, absently handing her the least soiled of his paint rags, for the anger had released the tears that grief and fear had held back. 'But why should you be looking for him here?'

'You *told* me he'd be here!' In her desperation, she rounded on Peter. 'You said he'd be here!' The dark wings of panic were beating wildly round her. 'And now we've wasted all this time, when we should have been out looking somewhere else.'

'See here, what's the fuss?' Rembrandt was bewildered, but game. 'Sit down and have a drink. There's no need to get upset. Denny is a sensible enough lad, he knows where he lives. It may be a bit naughty of him to stray off without saying anything at this hour of the night, but you really needn't worry all that much. He'll go back home when he's ready.'

'If he *can*,' Sheila said, and the tears flooded out anything else she might have said. She was aware that, over her head, Rembrandt's and Peter's eyes consulted briefly. Then Peter gave a quick jerk of his head and they both retreated to the far corner of the room. It was almost funny, the way everyone was trying to spare her, after she'd lived a lifetime with it all and knew everything that could be said; imagined every horror that could have been imagined. Except this final one.

No matter how low they kept their voices, words drifted to her. They were all words she had heard before, but she had still to learn to associate them with Mum and Denny. 'Sleeping pills . . . do away with . . . attempted suicide . . . mitigating circumstances . . . manslaughter . . .' And, 'Good God!' from Rembrandt, genuinely shaken.

She stiffened her backbone, dabbing at her eyes, breathing deeply. The brief spasm of tears had helped, she felt stronger now, ready to take up the search again. But where?

'I still don't understand –' they were walking back to her, Rembrandt grim, but still puzzled – 'why you came here. What made you think Denny might be with me? So far as I know, he has no idea where I live.'

'This.' Peter pulled the stub of tawny-gold chalk from his pocket and held it out. 'Denny was drawing squiggles on his bedside table with it. They appear to be the last thing he did before leaving the house. I thought it might point to what he'd had in mind. I knew you'd given him a lot of bits of chalk like this, and so – ' he faced Sheila apologetically – 'I guessed wrongly. I thought he was coming here.'

'That's mine, all right.' Rembrandt took the pastel stub and turned it round in his fingers. 'Squiggles, you say. What sort of squiggles?' He snatched up a canvas, reversed it, and scrawled rapidly on the back. 'Like that?'

'Well . . .' They both considered the scrawls carefully. Peter looked to Sheila, he'd been misled by the chalk itself, it hadn't occurred to him that the drawing might be meant to represent something.

'More or less,' Sheila decided, trying to visualize the original scrawls, before Aunt Vera had started to obliterate them. 'Yes, they looked like that.'

'I see.' Whistling between his teeth, Rembrandt stood there, frowning at the canvas, tossing the bit of chalk up into the air and catching it again. 'In that case, he didn't have me on his mind. That's my cocker spaniel ear, and this is the chalk for it. Denny was thinking about dogs – perhaps he went out to find one.'

It was possible. It was only too possible. Dismayed, Sheila thought of the long procession of dogs which had 'followed' Denny home. He'd always longed for one. But which one? And where would he go to get it?

'Dogs,' she said bleakly. 'Dogs. Where does that leave us? The city is full of dogs.'

'We might try the Dogs' Home.' Rembrandt was shrugging into a duffle coat, completely sober now, and beginning to share their desperate urgency as he realized the enormity of the situation. 'It's a start.'

'Would it be open at this hour?'

'Would Denny know the difference?' he asked.

'He'd never even think of such a thing,' she acknowledged sadly. Denny, acting on an impulse, would never stop to consider that places might be open or closed. He'd just go plunging along, to be astonished and rather hurt to find things weren't working out the way he planned them. Only, this time, he could be more than hurt – he could be dead. Curled up in a doorway nearby, to wait until the place opened in the morning, not knowing that, for him, morning wasn't going to come.

'I saw him with a dog today,' Peter remembered suddenly. 'A puppy. I had the impression he was going to let it out of its garden and play with it. He stopped, though, when he saw me. He might have gone back there tonight.'

'Where?' Sheila asked quickly.

'Quite a way from here,' Peter admitted. 'In the other direction. If he went there, then I've brought you completely out of the way. I'm sorry.'

She wondered vaguely if that dreadful sinking feeling were going to be a part of her for the rest of her life. Probably. It was something she was going to have to learn to live with. Like so many other things. Things she didn't want to think about right now, couldn't face. Any more than she could face inactivity, however momentary. She moved restlessly.

'Let's go, then. If we hurry – '

'We're not sure he's there,' Rembrandt reminded her. 'He might have gone to the Dogs' Home. He might have gone to quite another place. We can't be sure.'

'I'll phone in,' Peter decided. 'They can send a patrol car to check that area quicker than we can get there.'

'Yes,' she said, curiously reluctant. After all, it didn't matter who found Denny, just so long as he was found. But strange men in police uniforms coming at him would frighten him. And you could never be sure what he'd do when he was frightened. He might decide to try to fight; more probably, he might run away and hide. Hide so well that he could not be found again – until it was too late.

'Have you a telephone?' Peter turned to Rembrandt.

'Sorry,' he said, 'we don't run to such luxuries around here. But there's an outside phone nearby. You can call from there – if the vandals haven't got at it.'

'Right!' Peter whirled, as though he, too, were unable to stand inactivity. 'Let's go.'

Rembrandt paused to snap off the lights.

'No!' Sheila cried, overwhelmed by the sudden feeling that too many lights were going out tonight. She could not bear the darkness.

'I mean,' she said, as they both looked at her, 'Denny *might* come here, after all. You never know. And if he finds the place in darkness, he'll go away again. But if there's a light on, he'll know you're coming back, and he'll wait for you.'

'True,' Rembrandt said, almost as though he knew what she really felt. He reversed the switch and light sprang into the room again. He closed the door quietly on the silent canvases and followed them up the stairs, leaving the dim hall light on, as well.

'It's this way.' Gaining the pavement level, Rembrandt took the lead, at a pace fast enough to suit even Sheila. The urgency of the situation seemed to be filtering through his quick artist's imagination. She felt he was sensitive to all the nuances which Peter had omitted in his swift potted version of the night's events. Also – she felt a faint warming glow – like Peter, he was a friend of Denny's.

The thought of the telephone drew her, yet repelled her. After Peter had used it to direct the search for Denny into a fresh direction, she must call the hospital. Ask how Mum was, find out if she were still alive. Either way, the answer must be almost more than she could bear.

If Mum had died, then she must live with the knowledge that it was partly her fault. She could never forget that – thinking she was being so clever, thinking that she was sparing Mum an ordeal – she had kept Vera from Mum's bedroom. Vera, who could recognize the difference between natural sleep and a coma. She had deliberately done everything in her power to prevent Vera from going near Mum. For the rest of her life, she must wonder whether that extra time would have meant the difference between life and death. Vera wouldn't hurl it in her teeth – give Vera that – it was she herself who would sit in unending judgement through long sleepless nights.

And if Mum lived – if she were to survive, and they failed to find Denny in time – what then? Attempted suicide wasn't a criminal offence any more. But murder was. Peter was already bearing down on all the conciliatory phrases: 'mitigating circumstances', 'diminished responsibility', 'manslaughter', that betrayed the way the law was thinking. And it was too late to try to hush anything up. The police, out searching for Denny, knew all about it. The solemn majesty of the law was already on the march. Would Mum have to stand trial? Go to prison?

'Just around the corner here,' Rembrandt said, and the telephone kiosk loomed out of the mist ahead of them.

Peter lengthened his stride, moving away from them. He was already dialling when they reached the kiosk. In another moment, he began to speak. Obviously, the phone was in working order.

He looked splendidly real and solid in the light of the kiosk. In contrast, she felt as insubstantial as the mist swirling about her. She leaned weakly against the building behind the telephone kiosk.

'Careful,' Rembrandt said, gently pulling her away from it, 'you'll get your coat all dirty.' As though she hadn't long ago passed into a world where such things were inconsequential. 'Someone's been playing silly b's with chalk around here.'

Absently, she focused on the thick chalk scrawls, while something about them tried to register on her exhausted brain. Inside, Peter looked out at her and made a hopeful grimace.

'Denny!' she cried. 'It's Denny!' Rembrandt looked at her oddly.

'Don't you see?' She gripped his arm earnestly. *'That's* what Denny drew on the bedside table.' She pointed to the curling hair, now recognizable as such. 'Denny's been this way tonight.'

'I see.' Rembrandt looked at the hair, and at the delicate profile limned beneath it.

'That,' he said decisively, 'is no cocker spaniel.'

DENNY

From the corner of the street, he had seen her in the lighted window, the bright beckoning glow of her hair unmistakable. He had just been going to wave when the bad man came and pulled her away.

He had to get to Merelda and help her. Denny straightened, pulling himself away from the supporting lamp-post and trying to force his lethargic legs to a faster pace. Merelda needed him.

It was certainly getting foggy. The road ahead of him blurred and wavered. Everything seemed hazy and unreal. He felt all wobbly, too. As though, when he put his feet down, there might not be any road underneath them, or they might not hold him up. He'd never felt so strange before.

It wasn't far now. He could make it. Her steps were the ones with the flower-pots at the top. And the key was underneath one of the flower-pots. It would be easy to find. He'd probably feel better, too, once he was inside the house. It would be warm in there, and there wouldn't be this fog getting in front of his eyes. He just had to keep going, not think about stopping to rest, and he'd be there.

The cement steps loomed up before him, looking steep and high enough to reach the sky. At the top, he sat down, breathing heavily.

The flower-pot was heavier than it looked, he had to use both hands to lift it. And then the key wasn't under it. Not that one. There were three along each side of the ledge enclosing the steps. All the same size, all heavy. As he looked at them, they blurred and receded. Fog was getting worse.

He rubbed his eyes, repressing a yawn, and the flower-pots reappeared sharply and clearly. Unsteadily, again with both hands, he lifted the next flower-pot and replaced it. Then the third, the one nearest the steps. The blurring fog rolled in again as he set the pot down and he missed the ledge. It rolled down the steps, shattering as it hit the pavement, spilling dirt across the cement like blood from a wound. He wondered if the poor plant was hurt, in pain – and then whether anyone had heard.

Fearfully, he glanced up at the lighted window, but no shapes moved behind it. A sound like thunder seemed to come from above. Vaguely, he distinguished drums and loud brass. Maybe they hadn't noticed anything, after all, if they were listening to noisy music.

The key was under the flower-pot nearest the door on the opposite wall. Had Merelda told him that? She might have. He couldn't always remember so well, and he couldn't always tell left from right, either.

He held his breath, fumbling to get the key into the lock – that was always the hardest part – and then the door swung open. As he stepped inside, the hall dipped and swirled about him. He stumbled, recovered himself quickly, and shut the door. It slipped out of his grasp and slammed, the noise hitting his eardrums with an almost physical pain. But no door opened at the head of the stairs, no grim figure stood there to demand what he thought he was doing.

He knew what he was doing, what he had yet to do. The study door was invitingly ajar and a dim light burned just inside. Merelda had left it on for him. His heart glowed at her thoughtfulness. Merelda was his friend. And he would help her, as she had asked. Then she would continue to be his friend, for ever.

Smiling, he went to the desk. Easing the drawer open, he groped inside for the gun. It was still there, as she had said it would be. He took it out with difficulty, his hands were beginning to seem as though they didn't belong to him. They weren't responding properly to the commands from his brain. His fingers curled awkwardly around the butt of the gun, giving him no assurance that they might not suddenly let it drop. The room grew darker and was unsteady again.

Without closing the drawer, he went back into the hallway. The stairs were straight ahead now and the drawing-room was behind the closed door at the top. Even as he looked at them, they seemed to grow steeper and higher.

He couldn't manage them carrying all this stuff, but Merelda had said he'd have to have the gun. He bent and deposited the airline bag at the foot of the stairs. Blackness swooped at him like a bat as he straightened up.

He clung to the stair rail until his head cleared. Then, slowly, he began to climb. He wished the music wasn't so loud and noisy. It hurt his head, the thunder on the drum vibrating through him, accentuating the heavy pulsing of his blood. The stairs were beginning to sway in evil rhythm with the drums, too. He'd never reach the top, it was like trying to go up a down escalator, no matter how many steps you took there still seemed to be the same endless number to go. He closed his eyes and that made it a little better. When you couldn't see how far you had to go, it didn't seem so bad.

The stairs lurched under him abruptly and he had to fight to open his eyes, they wanted to stay closed. He had reached the top. He shifted the gun to his right hand and stood there, staring at the closed door.

He wanted to sit down on the top step and rest a while. He wanted it more than he could remember wanting anything in his whole life. More than a puppy dog, even. Much, much more than being home in his own bed – that had been earlier. Now, he was so far from home, in distance and in time, that it might have been just a pleasant dream he'd had once. The reality was here, in the aching weariness, all the things he still had to do, and the shadows reaching out to close around him.

He crossed to the door and leaned against the wall beside it. Even that little had cost him nearly as much energy as climbing the stairs. Maybe it wouldn't matter if he sat down and sort of rested for a few minutes before –

On the other side of the door, a woman screamed. Or was it something to do with the music – a singer hitting a high note? He couldn't be sure. But Merelda was behind that door with the bad man. He couldn't rest now – maybe she was being hurt.

He fumbled for the door knob, but it slipped away from his grasp. He had to try again, pushing at the door as he did so. Then, abruptly, he was in the room with them. Blinking in the bright light, he brought the gun up to point at the man.

They were both on the couch, Merelda leaning back against the cushions, the man's hand at her throat. They froze as they saw him.

'You leave her alone!' he blurted. 'You stop hurting her!'

They seemed to move in slow motion. The man withdrew his hand, Merelda turned her head. Very carefully, they levered themselves to a sitting position. The woman's voice screamed again – it was coming from the record machine.

'I –' The man swallowed and spoke in a cautious, conciliatory tone, his eyes on the gun. 'I'm not hurting her, lad.'

'You're not?' Denny asked uncertainly.

'I wouldn't hurt her for the world. She's my wife – you know that, don't you? I love her.'

'You do?' Denny looked at him in confusion. He didn't seem like a bad man. Not like Merelda had said. He wondered if he'd got the right man. But this was the man who had pulled her away from the window, had had his hands round her neck. Still uncertain, he turned to Merelda.

'Why, Denny . . .' Her face lit with a welcome only he could see. 'What a surprise. What are you doing here? And –' her eyes slid sideways to look at her husband – 'and where did you get that gun?'

'In the desk,' he said simply. 'It was right where you said it was.'

'What's that?' The man whirled on Merelda. 'Were you fool enough to –?'

'Don't you touch her,' Denny said quickly. 'You leave her alone!' He waved the gun, reinforcing his commands.

'I'm not touching her.' The man subsided, his eyes darting from the gun to the expanse of carpet separating him from Denny.

'Then don't.' Denny began to feel vaguely pleased. It was all going the way Merelda had said. The man was scared. Now, what else was it he had to do? Oh, yes.

'Promise,' he said. 'Promise you won't hurt her again.'

'I never hurt her,' the man said. 'I've never raised a finger to her.' He looked at the pointing gun again and abandoned argument. 'All right,' he said, 'if it will make you feel better, I promise. I've never hurt her – and I never will.'

'That's good.' Denny lowered the gun. He looked at Merelda in elation, waiting for her praise. He'd helped her, saved her. Now they could all be friends.

But Merelda was frowning. And she seemed so far away. The whole room seemed remote, misty and swaying. What was the matter?

'Oh, Merelda.' He sank into a chair, blackness swooping around him again. 'Merelda, I feel awful.'

SHEILA

Peter finished his call and rang off. He came out of the telephone kiosk to stare at the sketch with them. 'They'll check the area where I saw Denny with the pup,' he said glumly. 'But, if he wasn't thinking about dogs –'

And he wasn't, they knew that now. He was thinking about women – probably one particular woman. And that meant – Sheila pressed her hand against her lips, battling the impulse to cry, to scream, neither of which would do Denny any good right now. That meant they were really lost – *he* was lost. Somewhere in this big city – on his way to some unknown woman.

And what about Mum? She ought to call the hospital. She started into the kiosk, but Peter put his hand on her arm, stopping her.

'There's no news,' he said. 'I asked. "Doing as well as

can be expected." That's all they'll ever tell you, anyway.'

'If I can get Aunt Vera,' she said, 'she might tell me more.' But she flinched from talking to Vera, from hearing the veiled eagerness in Vera's voice when she enquired about Denny. From the false heartiness that would assure her, 'Everything's going to be all right'; knowing that, for her and Vera, 'all right' meant two different things. It was all right with Aunt Vera if Denny died.

She allowed Peter to draw her away from the door. They went back to staring hopelessly at the sketch on the wall – it told them so much, and so little.

And yet, there was something it ought to tell her. She tried to concentrate her mind, push Mum into the background. Mum was already in hospital, everything possible being done for her; talking to Matron, or Aunt Vera, wouldn't change anything. It was Denny they had to think about now. Denny.

She tried to think back. To earlier today, aeons ago, the world on the other side of the chasm, when everything had been calm and safe and normal, when getting the tea ready on time had been the heaviest problem she had to face.

Tea. And Denny, sitting at the table, smiling and happy, and trying to confide something to her in his inarticulate way. But half her mind had been on Mum, worrying about what the doctor would tell her. She hadn't been paying much attention to Denny's wanderings. But he had said something –

'Is she local?' Rembrandt asked. The two men were still squinting at the sketch.

'Hard to tell.' Peter turned his torch on the drawing, holding it close, as though additional light might tell him something more. 'It isn't much of a portrait, you know.'

'It's as good as you could get with your Identikit,' Rembrandt argued. 'You ought to be trained to distinguish suspects at a glance.'

'If I've seen them before,' Peter said. 'What about your artist's eye? And you work this area a lot. If she's local, perhaps you've seen her before.'

'*If* she's local,' Rembrandt said. They both stared

soberly at the drawing.

'The river!' It came back to Sheila suddenly. 'Denny said he'd been to tea this afternoon with a pretty lady who lived along the river.'

'It's a long river,' Rembrandt said slowly.

'But Denny passed this way.' Peter turned towards the river. 'There's no pathway downriver from here, it's cut off by playing fields. That means he must be heading upriver. It's a residential district, plenty of houses and blocks of flats.'

They began walking towards the river. Sheila tried to be calm – it was ridiculous to hope. Just because the search had narrowed a bit. It was still a long river, as Rembrandt had pointed out – and Denny, with his long loping stride, could cover a lot of territory in an hour or so. There was no knowing how much of a head start he had on them. He could be anywhere by this time.

Where was he going? And what did he think he was going to do when he got there?

'Her name was Merelda!' Sheila remembered. Neither Peter nor Rembrandt reacted. The name was no help to them.

They turned a corner and were at the river. It flowed, dark and deep, below the embankment on the opposite side of the street. Along this side, a row of town houses looked out over the misty depths. They were blank and anonymous, giving no clue to the identity of their occupants. Denny could be inside any one of them.

Or he could be lying in a heap in some shadowed doorway, or on the river bank. The street itself was deserted, except for themselves.

'I'll just check.' Peter left them, crossing the street to flash his torch over the wall. 'All clear to the end of the row,' he reported, coming back to them.

A cold wind blew in off the river, carrying the mist before it. Sheila was not the only one who shivered, and the increasing chill had nothing to do with it. The street stretched endlessly along the river, at least a mile to the next bridge. After a brief giving way to the commercial district crouched at the end of the bridge, the residences took over again, continuing for miles. What chance had they of finding Denny in time?

They began walking, by tacit consent, down the street, towards the distant bridge, Sheila between the two men. Not too quickly, their urgency slowed by the need to look twice at each clump of black shadows, eyes probing to make certain no human form lay curled there.

They passed one cross-street, then another. The row of houses immediately ahead had something odd about it, struck a jarring note not instantly discernible. There was just a certain disorder about it which reminded one instinctively of Denny. Sheila quickened her steps, the others kept pace.

Midway down the row, a flower-pot lay shattered at the foot of a flight of steps. Other flower-pots flanked a doorway in tipsy array. Denny's handiwork? They stopped in front of the house, staring up at it.

'A dog,' Rembrandt said uncertainly, 'or a cat. It doesn't prove anything.' They would have to go inside to prove anything. Ask questions. They were not quite prepared to take those steps yet. The evidence was indicative, but not conclusive.

'The dog –' Peter turned his torch on the doorway – 'left his key in the latch.'

'Shine that torch down here,' Rembrandt directed suddenly, squatting to look at something. The beam swung down to illumine a yellow chalk squiggle on the bottom step.

'He's been this way,' Rembrandt said. 'Whether he's in this house, or not – ?' He shrugged.

'At least, we can ask.' Sheila started up the steps.

The men were staring after her, indecisive about following, when the first shot rang out upstairs.

The second shot shattered the picture window above their heads.

MERELDA

The imbecile! The great overgrown lout! What was he doing? What was wrong with him? He slumped in the big armchair, his eyes opening and closing, shaking his head dazedly. Was he going to fall asleep right in the middle of the scene? Or be sick?

Behind her, she felt Keith stir, his muscles tensed as he edged forward. If he got to that gun first . . .

'Stay still,' she whispered. 'You'll set him off again. Let me deal with it. He thinks I'm his friend.'

'Be careful, lass.' Keith caught her arm to hold her back. 'You can't tell what he'll do. He's not just daft – he's raving mad with it.'

'It will be all right,' she said softly. 'I can get closer to him than you can. He trusts me.'

So did Keith. She smiled as he released her arm. 'Be careful,' he said again. 'If anything happens to you, I'll kill that maniac.'

You aren't going to be in a position to kill anyone. The thought was so exhilarating she nearly voiced it aloud. But not yet. Not until she had her hand on the gun.

'Merelda?' Denny opened his eyes, searching for her, without seeming to see her. 'Merelda? Everything's all funny. I don't feel good.' He slumped lower in the chair. 'I want my mother.'

'It's all right, Denny,' she cooed. 'I'm right here. I'll help you.' She slid off the couch and started towards him, cautiously enough to reassure Keith; smoothly enough to encourage Denny.

'Merelda?' Once more the curiously blank gaze travelled past her. 'Merelda, it's so dark here.' His hand, as though unaware it still held the gun, came up to rub at his eyes, his forehead.

Keith, scenting an enemy's disadvantage, rose to his feet and started forward, ignoring her signal to stay where he

was. She tried to wave him back, but he kept advancing
steadily.

'Stop that!' she said sharply. 'You're frightening me!' As
she had hoped, each man thought she was speaking to
the other.

'You leave her alone!' Denny reacted immediately, bringing the wavering gun to aim in Keith's general direction.
Keith froze, only his eyes moving as he sought an opening.

'Steady on, lad,' Keith said. 'Steady.' The effect was
unsteadying.

Denny struggled to his feet, his mind unreeling to the
beginning of the scene, to the task he had come here to
perform. 'You hurt her,' he accused. 'You frightened her.
You're a bad man!'

'That's right, Denny.' Merelda drew closer to him, speaking low, hypnotically. Keith was too far away to hear. He
still watched her hopefully, waiting for her to charm the
gun out of Denny's hand.

'He shouts at me, Denny, and he hits me sometimes.
And, look –' she pulled at the lace hanging loose at her
neckline – 'he tore my gown, too. Just before you got here.
You saved me, Denny. You're going to save me again,
aren't you?'

'Bad man. Bad, bad man.' The room began to dip and
sway. His knees felt wobbly. He'd thought it was all over,
that he'd successfully frightened the bad man before and
won his promise to stop hurting Merelda. But the man was
trying to come nearer – to take the gun away from him –
perhaps to hurt Merelda again. Bad men didn't keep
promises.

'Keep back.' He waved the gun. 'Keep away. You stop
hurting her.'

'Where did he get this wild idea?' the man demanded
plaintively. 'What makes him think I've been mistreating
you, lass?'

She ignored him. It was nothing but a ghost speaking – or
soon would be. He was already dead, he just didn't realize
it. Only the final step remained.

'Denny.' She stood beside him now, close enough to

put one hand on his shoulder, steadying him. What was
wrong with him? He had nearly blown the whole scene.
Not to worry, it didn't matter now. He was here, the gun
was here. And Keith was standing there, on the wrong side
of the gun . . . waiting.

'Denny . . .'

He turned his head – it seemed to have grown too big and
heavy for his body – towards her. Then, sensing movement
from the man, turned back. It was getting harder to hold
up the gun, he hoped the man didn't notice this.

'Merelda,' he whined, 'I want to go home. I feel awful.'
He'd told her that before. Why wasn't she paying any
attention? Merelda was his friend, wasn't she?

'It's all right, Denny,' she cooed. 'It's almost over, and
then you can go home. There's just one more little thing
you have to do. You know that, don't you? We talked
about it.'

'Do . . . ?' The lights were so funny, they kept going on
and off. It didn't seem to bother the others, but it was
making him dizzier. He tried to concentrate on what
Merelda was saying. She seemed to want something more
from him, something else he had to do. 'What . . . ?'

'*You* know, Denny.' Her voice was soft, insinuating. He
struggled to comprehend. He was disappointing her in
some way, he knew. He didn't want that.

'He won't keep his promise, Denny. He never keeps his
promises. You've got to make him stop. For good. Help me,
Denny. There's only you to save me. You're my friend,
aren't you, Denny?'

'Yes.' He grasped thankfully at that, the one sure point
in all the fog and darkness. 'Yes, Merelda, I am.'

'Then – shoot! Shoot him!' Her voice rose, her hand
pressed down on his shoulder urgently. '*Use* the gun – I
showed you how. Shoot him – kill him!'

'By God!' the man said. 'By God!' He leaped forward.

Denny struggled to pull the trigger, but his fingers were
nerveless. Even the hand holding the gun was betraying
him, trying to drop down to his side. He could feel Merelda
grabbing at the gun. The man loomed up in front of him

like some creature from a nightmare, elongated, shadowy, menacing. The room gave one final, terrible lurch and he dissolved into the swooping blackness.

'All right,' Merelda said. 'All right, then *I* will!' She hurled herself at Denny's drooping arm, forcing it up, her hand curling over his on the gun.

'Lass, you've gone mad! Stop it. It's all right now. He's passed out.' Keith was babbling at her. Just what you might expect from him. No dignity in the face of death, no memorable last words. What use his money and his power now?

He closed with Denny, fighting both of them for the gun. His pleading eyes met her triumphant ones and she had the satisfaction of seeing full knowledge of the situation register in them. He knew now.

'You told this poor daftie about the gun,' he said. 'You told him I mistreated you. You deliberately worked on him to –' Even then, he couldn't quite say it, still avoided the admission. He twisted at the gun with both hands, so did she. Face to face, they battled for possession, but Denny's inert hand still clung tenaciously to it.

'I hate you,' she gasped. 'I've hated you for years!' They renewed their struggle for the gun. Denny gave a convulsive movement, returned to semi-consciousness by the battle raging around him – throwing them both off balance. The first shot rang out.

She saw Keith's face go blank with shock. Until then, the fool had still been fighting to believe she didn't mean it. For good measure, she fired again. But, so near her goal, triumph had unsteadied her and the shot went wild, shattering the picture window.

Denny crashed to the ground, dragging her down with him. They dropped the gun. Keith had stepped back, staring down at them both incredulously. He would fall next.

The shots would bring the neighbours, the police. She lay where she had fallen, it would be a nice tableau for them to discover. The loyal wife, overcome while struggling with the hulking brute who had killed her dear husband. But why didn't Keith fall?

The room had cooled rapidly, the chill of the river mist swirling into it through the broken window. It was amazing how cold it had become so swiftly.

Keith still remained standing . . . perhaps one more bullet . . . just to make sure. She groped for the gun, but her hand was already numbed by the cold, she couldn't close it round the gun.

'Lass, lass – ' He dropped now, to his knees beside her. 'Eh, lass – ' Tears were in his eyes. She tried to move away as he reached out for her, but felt curiously inert. Perhaps it didn't matter.

'Eh, lass – ' He pulled her free of Denny, cradling her in his arms. 'I tried to give you everything any woman could want. I thought you were happy – '

There was blood on his shirt now. She smiled in faint satisfaction at seeing it. 'I . . .' But her voice wasn't quite strong enough. Her lips seemed numb. Along with the growing coldness in the room, there seemed to be an increasing darkness, as well. She tried again. 'I . . .'

'Shhh, be still. Save your strength.' He raised his head, listening to footsteps racing up the stairs. 'Help's coming. We'll get a doctor for you – '

'Me. . . ?' He had it wrong. He was the one who needed a doctor, something she must delay until it was too late to do any good. She struggled feebly to get up . . . feebly.

'No . . .' Her hands fluttered, trying to explore. There was no pain, no consciousness of a wound. Only the coldness . . . and the dark.

'Easy, love, easy.' Tears were streaming down his face. That was what convinced her.

Even now, a wave of irritation swept her, he still didn't understand. He'd rearrange the facts until they became his own kind of truth. Something he could continue to live with. If she could not finish him, at least she would destroy that.

'I . . . hate . . . you . . .' Her voice was stronger, she watched him wince as the words hit him. 'I tried . . . to kill you . . . I tried . . . my best . . .'

'It's all right, love.' He stroked her hair. The fool thought she was apologizing. 'It's all right. Happen women get strange fancies at a time like this.'

A time like this . . . Her eyes blurred, she fought against it. *Time* . . . How could this happen to her? She was too young, she had too much to live for. It was Keith who ought to be lying here, dying, to free her for the wonderful life that would stretch ahead of her as a young, healthy widow.

'Get a doctor!' Keith snapped out the order to someone she could not see, someone who stood in the doorway. It was too much effort to turn her head. She tried to say something and heard herself moan faintly instead.

'Hang on, lass,' he said. 'Hang on, love. We'll pull you through. You're going to be all right. You're both going to be all right.'

Then she knew what he meant, realized what he had been thinking. *A time like this* . . . She pulled herself away from him with the last of her strength.

'You fool!' she said. In this last rally, her voice was high and clear. 'You fool! Did you think I'd have . . . *your* child?'

SHEILA

Shards of glass showered on to the pavement, just missing them. They didn't hesitate any longer. Turning the key, Peter pushed the door open and they rushed into the hallway. .

There, at the foot of the stairs, was Denny's familiar airline bag. The shots had come from upstairs.

'Oh, God! Oh, Denny!' Sheila started forward, but Rembrandt pulled her back.

'We'll go first. Keep well behind us.'

They were trying to protect her, to shield her from the scene that might be waiting behind that door at the top of the stairs. Sheila followed so closely she was nearly treading on their heels. Intent on what lay ahead, the men paid no further attention.

She was looking over their shoulders when the door opened. Directly opposite, the broken window gaped into blackness. At first, there seemed to be no people in the room. Then she saw them – they were all on the floor.

'Denny!' Heedless of danger, she pushed Rembrandt and Peter aside and ran to him. He lay huddled near the fire. The shots did not appear to have touched him. He was still breathing, in the same strange way Mum had been. But more lightly. He moved and groaned when she tugged at him.

'*Get a doctor!*' At first, she thought she'd said the words, they were so prominent in her mind. Then she realized someone else had spoken. Still intent on Denny, she sensed, rather than saw, Rembrandt leave the room. Peter came forward.

'What's happened here?'

'Hang on, love.' She saw the man, then, kneeling on the floor, holding a woman in his arms, talking to her softly. He ignored Peter, ignored everyone but the woman. Blood stained the ruffles and lace of her negligee. That was where the other shot had gone.

Denny stirred and she lost interest in everything else in the room. 'Denny! Denny!' As Aunt Vera had done with Mum, she slapped his face lightly. He whimpered and his eyelids twitched. His head rolled away from her protestingly.

'Denny! Denny!' She shook him. He responded further, encouraging her. Perhaps he hadn't taken as much of the cocoa as Mum had, or there hadn't been so much barbiturate in his cup. Also, he was a lot bigger and that made a difference, didn't it? A stronger dosage would be needed to still his heavy frame.

Across from them, the woman raised her head, shouted out something – something about a child – and then her head fell back against the man's arm, her eyes not quite closed, but no longer seeing anything.

'Wha . . .?' The woman's voice reached Denny, got through to him as her own had not. He lifted his head, struggling to one elbow, and opened his eyes, looking over at her. 'Merelda?' Throwing off Sheila as though she had not been there, he rolled to his hands and knees, crawling over to crouch beside the woman.

Sheila watched uncomprehendingly. Who were these people? How had Denny got mixed up with them? What had happened here?

The man was crying openly. Tears of sympathy rolled down Denny's face. The man was still stroking the bright shining hair. Denny's hand crept out uncertainly towards the shimmering head. He touched it gently.

The man looked up at Denny. 'Eh, lad,' he said. 'You loved her, too.'

DENNY

Sheila was singing in the kitchen. Sheila sang a lot these days. She called out something to Mum and Mum answered, laughing. Mum laughed a lot these days. Even Aunt Vera was nicer than she used to be.

It was something to do with the long, long time that Mum had been away in hospital. She'd had an operation and whatever was wrong wasn't as wrong as everybody had thought. And she was like herself again and didn't get upset so easily any more.

He'd been in hospital himself – just for a few days, they said. He hadn't had an operation, though – he didn't know what he'd had. It was a time he couldn't remember very clearly. Just a swooping blackness and the voices. ('*Denny, Denny . . . you're my friend, Denny . . . you'll help me, Denny . . .*') And the awful feeling that he had to push himself on, because there was something he had to do. ('*It was all a bad dream, Denny. Forget it, Denny. Don't bother your head about it, Denny.*')

Constable Peter was coming to dinner. He came to the house often now. So did Rembrandt. They were good friends. They took him out to the films and on picnics – and they let Sheila come, too. They were better friends than ever, these days.

Only, once, hadn't there been another friend? A different kind of friend? Soft, shining hair and Madonna face; low, trusting voice. ('*You'll help me, Denny. You'll save me, Denny.*') Or had that all been part of a dream? That long, confused dream of a pretty lady.

Had it really been a dream? There were times when it still seemed so real that he could almost see her again and see the house she took him to. Soon after he got out of hospital, he'd gone looking for it along the river.

He'd found it, too, although it didn't look quite the same. The plants in the five earthenware flower-pots were dead, just twigs, with a few rustling leaves attached, sticking up out of dry cracked dirt. The big upstairs window was boarded up. There was a 'FOR SALE' sign on a tilting post. It didn't look as though anyone had lived there for a long, long time. And yet, it was the right house, wasn't it?

He'd stood there, frowning up at the boarded window, as though it could tell him something, if it would. And then Constable Pete had come by and found him. ('*Come along, Denny. That's just an empty house. The owners have gone away. They won't be coming back.*') And he and Pete had gone and had an ice-cream.

But, just for a moment, there had been something he'd almost remembered, standing there. Something about two shining colours: a tawny-gold and a dark, sticky, wet red. And a bad man, who didn't seem bad, somehow, and who was crying. But that proved it was a dream, didn't it? Big boys don't cry. (Even though sometimes, like now, trying to think about it, to remember the lost dream, the lost time, he wanted to.)

'Denny, Denny.' Sheila was calling at the back door. 'Denny, come in and wash before dinner. Peter will be here any minute.'

'Coming!' He waved, then it was his turn to call. 'Here, Fritz! Come on, boy. Time to go in now.'

A bush quivered and shook and a golden cocker spaniel

puppy bounded out of it. Denny watched, his heart expanding with the pride of ownership as the puppy ran straight to him. Mum and Sheila had given in, at last, given Fritz to him for his very own. And he was one smart puppy, he knew his master already, and he obeyed commands. When spring came again, they could go running in the park. He was the smartest dog in the neighbourhood, in the whole world, maybe. And he was little yet. Just wait until he was a big grown-up dog.

Denny leaned over to pull fondly at a soft, tawny-gold ear. The puppy yelped enthusiastically and twisted to lick his hand.

Rembrandt was going to give him more drawing lessons, too, so that he could sketch Fritz as he was growing up and have lots of pictures – nicer than photographs. Rembrandt had given him a box of chalks for his very own – whole chalks, too. (*Things are looking up, my lad. What a successful show will do! Oh, not a raving success – but enough, enough. Enough to get me in off the pavement and start me up the ladder.*)

Sheila had helped with Rembrandt's show. Denny had gone one afternoon when it wasn't very crowded, but he hadn't liked looking at the scarey paintings. He'd watched Sheila and Rembrandt laughing together, instead. She laughed that way with Constable Pete, too.

(And another dream had begun to grow. A laughing, happy dream, with Sheila marrying one of his good friends, and all of them living together happily ever after. It was a dream that might come true, too. He didn't know which one would be nicer, Rembrandt or Constable Pete. Maybe Sheila didn't know, either. But there was lots of time to decide.)

'DENNY!'

'I'm coming!' He began running towards the house with long, loping strides. At his feet, the golden spaniel scampered to keep up with him.